LEGEND

The Tale of the Biggest Revolution Ever!

JAAZIB SHERAZ

Thanks to:

My teacher, for the last six years, who taught me everything. The man who deserves the greatest love, praise, and admiration of all the students. The man of humour, intellect, and empathy, **Mr. Rayees Ahmad Raina**, faculty of English. I am extremely grateful for his priceless contribution to this publication.

My friends, who were eager to know about my work, were always excited about all the news that I gave them about this work.

My parents, who never refused anything. Who always supported me and helped me in the toughest times.

And finally, YOU. A person who wants revolution and a great nation.

Thank you!

Contents

Contents

Prologue

Well, people say that good people don't remain for much time. And well, I believed that it is true. Really, like tell me some names and you will be done. But when we talk about those who have done bad, they remain and they exist. They actually rule the people. The greatest lie is that truth is the most powerful weapon and evilness is much bad and harmful. So, we should be positive to bring changes and never do evil for the sake of goodness. But what happens when you do both? What happens when you do 'bad' for the good? What happens when you kill someone for someone?

I was walking through a narrow lane. I wanted to bring some milk from the shop. There was already a big queue in a small shop. Why don't people just go to supermarkets and leave me alone here? Meanwhile, I was waiting; I was lost in my dreams. I thought about how good it would have been if you could get services from robots? But at the same time, another thought struck me that if robots work, where will humans go? Well, these debates happened in my mind frequently. Just another normal day for me. I was fed up with the line. One person was taking an average of fifteen minutes for nothing! I decided to move to another shop.

I started moving. I saw a big, wide road, two-way just in front of me. It was actually the end of the narrow lane. I entered the big road. It felt odd. It was like entering a world of light from the darkness of streets.

I saw many poor beggars on the road. Most of them were children. They seemed very hungry and poor. Well, I didn't have any money to give them. If I did so, then my mom would have no property to give me. I had to buy milk, that was the goal. I ignored them and moved on. I knew a big store nearby.

"Tumhe dillagi bhool jaane…" I was singing to myself when I saw the big store. It was on the other side of the road. I tried to cross the road while singing more and more. There were many chances that a car might hit me. Well, if I die, my mother would kill me. I didn't expect that. I didn't want to die at such a tender age. Yes, I am young, really young. I might be young, but my thoughts are no less special than Chetan Bhagat himself. He is my favourite writer after all.

I entered the store. It felt cool inside, maybe due to an AC. I didn't care. It also had that usual store cold smell. It is normal. The shopkeeper saw me with his one eye on me and the other on his diary. I don't know what poems he is writing from debts and credits. However, I went backside.

Luck does not wait and look for you. It is just as it is. Anything can happen, anytime. Life can play bad games with you. Maybe mad also. Everyone's life jokes with him (and her, to be less Racist, of course!). Well, my life was also ready to prank me harshly. This world is unexpected. A bullet can hit you anytime; well, I didn't get hit but what happened was not even less than that.

"Why are you gloomy, sir?" I asked a man who was lying down with such a gloomy face that you can think of those old dying cancer patients from TV ads.

"Who are you, kid?" he replied harshly, emphasising the last word correctly.

"I am—just leave that, sir. Why are you sad?" I asked again, expecting a good reply.

"Who are you? Just get lost!" he said even more harshly. I was offended.

"Sir, maintain your language!" I replied harshly as well.

"Wait a minute, who are you to tell me what I should do?" he said in an odd way. His eyeballs were about to burst.

"Listen, sir. I am not ordering you; I was just asking…"

"GO TO HELL, KID!" he interrupted and made my blood boil.

"Hey mister! Don't you dare to talk to me like that! I can send you to jail right now!" I said confidently, yet with a scary feeling in my heart.

He stood up and shocked me. He was taller than me even when my friends said that I am very tall.

"What?" he said, maybe showing superiority, but I respected his superiority.

"Sir, I was telling you that you look so educated and healthy. Can you tell me why the sun is setting so early?" I replied in metaphor and gave an odd grin.

"Hmmm! Well, boy, you seem clever," he said and smiled.

"Thank you, sir!" I replied with some kind of feeling of light-heartedness and a moment of pride for my timely reply.

"Well, kid, I am here for someone for my story," he said with an upset mood.

"Which story, sir?" I asked.

"Well, the story of my grandfather's brother!" he replied proudly.

"Isn't it too old a story like…"

"Kid, you don't know who my grandfather's brother was," he replied. "He was a legend."

"Well, why are you sitting inside a store?" I asked, diverting from the topic.

"I am tired. No one wants to write about him, you know!" he said with an even sadder face.

"Why?" I asked curiously.

"Because he was the most wanted criminal in India," he stated as if he was in a stand-up comedy show (even though he was sitting at the time).

Well, what was that? I am with a man whose, whoever was the biggest criminal, well, I was done, I guess.

"What?" I said in surprise and reflex.

"Yes, that is the reason," he continued.

"Well, can you tell me about your grandfather's brother?"

"Why should I tell you?" he demanded. Well, he was right. Why the hell would he tell me? And why the hell did I ask him? Well, just because I became curious and you know.

"I can write a novel," I said with full confidence.

"Can you even write your answers in the exam?" he said, busting me. I know I would have teared up a bit, but I couldn't cry because my tears wouldn't come up.

"Just trust me, sir. I can. I might seem little, well, I am, but I can write well," I said with a bit of confidence.

"Just leave," he said, and again, was lost in dreams.

"You know one thing, I first thought that your, whoever was the biggest criminal of India, so I should leave you for good. But then, it struck me that why the hell should I leave if I don't know the reason. I thought that if I get a hint, then I will write. Not for myself but for everyone, if they think that your whoever was a bat, sorry, bad man. I wanted to use this opportunity for me as well as for you.

"But you don't trust me. Of course, you will not because I am a kid, after all. But, I know what to write and how to write. So, I expect something brave from you. I want your trust, time, and truth. I think that I am capable of narrating a grand tale. Please do not underestimate me and give me this golden moment for my people and for you, please."

Maybe this had done the magic.

"Sit down and let me tell you what happened. Write, just try to write. No one wants to, but you want to. I don't trust you, but listen and write. I will analyse what you have written, and then I will tell you what to do," he said with an even brighter face.

"Thank you, sir. I will write it in the best way possible and bring a change in India…" I stopped. I thought I was going too far.

"What will you keep the title?" he asked.

"I will tell you after you tell me what happened. Come with me to the park."

PART 1

1

The Unknown Man

The car was moving at a decent speed along the beautiful hillsides of Himachal Pradesh. The driver was in a serious mood. The assistant was just waiting for the silent man to talk. He seemed to be very serious and moody. The man sitting in the front, adjacent to the driver, was thinking about himself rather than even thinking of others and looked very arrogant. The route was very long, heading to Delhi. Everyone was exhausted except the silent man, who was sitting comfortably at the back. His window was open, and air was coming in with great pressure. He was wearing a black formal suit with a brown leather bag. No one could bear the silence. The man had not spoken a word since they left their place.

Finally, the assistant broke the silence and said, "Sir, why did you choose this work?"

The man smiled and asked, "Why did you choose this work?" The assistant felt guilty to speak.

The man was feeling fresh when the assistant asked, "Sir, what is your real name?" The man remained silent and did not even look at him. The assistant seemed disappointed but wanted to make him talk. He knew something that might be shocking if it were true. He could have persuaded him to open the chamber of secrets.

The driver, who was driving a cart, said, "Well, Manoj is your son all right now?"

Manoj, the assistant, was confused and replied, "Which…" but suddenly looked in the mirror where he saw the driver making faces. He understood everything and continued, "Which cure are you talking about, brother? He is not even getting better!"

The man listened to them patiently and noticed everything. The man seemed to enjoy the views, and the driver was tired. They were sitting in a Fortuner, black in colour, shining and moving swiftly through the hills. The weather was just amazing. The road was a bit dangerous, but everyone managed to be calm. There were many cars also, but this car was different. All the cars had a number plate of Himachal Pradesh except that one. It had a red-coloured note at the front mirror, The Govt. of India. All the cars were moving a bit faster than they were.

"Why the hell are you slow?" the man said in a hoarse voice. "Can't you just move fast and make us reach fast?"

They were all bored. They had been travelling for around four hours straight. The assistant was thinking of food when the driver said, "*Saab,* can we eat somewhere quickly?"

Manoj was happy and thinking about food when he heard something that led his mood down again.

"Why?" the man asked with an odd attitude.

"We were feeling a bit hungry," stated innocent Manoj, the targeted assistant.

"We or you?" smiled the man.

The driver remained silent, and he already had the answer from the man. The assistant was going mad with him. He had worked with many but had never seen someone like him before, the first time in his life. Arrogant, austere, and not so benevolent.

The man smiled after some time and said, "Stop at that *dhaba.*"

Manoj felt like heaven. He was eagerly waiting for the car to stop. He had been bearing his hunger for the last two hours.

The car stopped at a *dhaba.* It was decent in size, and the manager seemed to be a Sikh with a red turban, *pagdi.* They parked the car outside the *dhaba.* Everyone was looking at the black Fortuner. It was like a giant among small people. It was a giant just likely the king of cars there. Everyone was looking at them.

Then two more cars followed them. They probably were with them and were their security. They stopped on the road. Some police personnel went down and some army. Everyone was shocked. They all saluted him. The assistant felt small but was happy with all that. They went and sat at a table. The army was outside and all people were still standing.

"Sit down, all. Why are you standing?" said the man and smiled at Manoj.

Everyone sat down. The servant brought some extra *chatni* for them. They had ordered *dal, roti, aanchar,* and some chatni, of course. They all were eating in a mess except the silent man and the guy who was sitting on the front seat. But they, after all, ate happily.

The man was happy after eating the food. He went to pay, but the assistant stopped him.

"Sir, you can't pay," he said, responsibly. "Let me pay, sir."

He agreed at first go, and Manoj was unsatisfied with him. Later, he was feeling regret for that. At first, the manager did not take the money, but after some tries, he took it and thanked the man.

"I gave the money, why are they thanking him instead?" Manoj thought with envy, because he dared not to talk in front of him.

❧

After they all ate, they left for the car. When everyone was in, they left with all cars following them. All the people on the way noticed them. They were now in the city of Shimla. They decided to stay the night there. They were looking for a hotel to stay. After some time of searching, they found one. Not so luxurious and regal, but they could manage there. It was medium-sized, made up of black bricks. It had French windows, and the chimney seemed to be the classic one. It was two-storied, and the lights at night made it shine like a jewel in black.

Manoj went to the hotel manager for the settlement.

"The price will be 5000 rupees per person," the manager said.

"Are you gone mad or what?" Manoj replied with disgust. "Are you a seven-star resort here?"

"Listen, man, this is the rate and this is what we take," he replied sharply. "Either pay or leave, for God's sake!"

"Do you even know who is with us?" said Manoj with great confidence.

"Whosoever it shall be, I don't care," replied the man coldly.

"We are with the collector *Saab*!" exclaimed Manoj in vain.

The man was out of his wits and could not think of anything. He sprang from his chair and headed towards the room of the man. He opened the door harshly and held the man's hands.

"Sir, we are pleased to have you here!" he remarked, but Manoj had thought that he would do something odd or bad to him. Like an unexpected cut with a machete! Leave it.

"I know, thank you!" the man replied with ego.

The manager served them tea, food, and took only 2000 Rupees per person, which he had accepted after bargaining for more than 5 minutes.

They spent the night there. The beds were comfortable, and the man had a very good night. Manoj was also thinking of the benefits of staying with such a person. He was full of powers, but he himself was a bit odd.

It was morning, and Manoj was already up. He thought to wake up the man, but when he went to his room, he found the door open. He was surprised. After some more examination, he found out that he was not even there. The man had already left somewhere. He peeped out of the window and saw that the man was already sitting in the car with the driver and the other man. They were ready to leave when he rushed harshly downwards. He was in haste and breathing heavily. They all laughed and invited him in. Manoj was not happy with the prank. They then left for the journey of two more days until Delhi.

They were in the car and saw the resort while leaving. It was diminishing, and they were watching it until it got lost. The focus then was only on the road and only the trip. The man was bored.

"Sir, why don't you really talk?" asked the man in the front seat. Manoj was also eager to listen, if only he spoke.

"Well, if you really want me to be..." suddenly the driver cleared his throat with a loud sound and everyone was looking at him awkwardly. "Ah, who I really am, then I can."

Manoj was accepting everything and was speaking from within. Everyone except the man at the front shouted loudly and waited for the real fun.

"Then do one thing," said the man.

"What!" replied the driver enthusiastically.

"Everyone, give me your phone," he pointed to the man on the front seat.

Without thinking, the driver and the assistant gave their phones, but the man took some time. Eventually, he handed it over. He looked very uncomfortable.

"Now this is my phone," the man said and breathed.

"Let me please connect the Bluetooth of my phone with the car,"

After he had connected the phone to the car, he was not going mad, but Manoj was. He turned on the music. They all were enjoying. They were moving their heads with the beats that followed. The road seemed more beautiful than the other day because of the songs and the real face of the man. After some time, it was now time for the lunch.

They left the car and then entered a restaurant that was good.

It was red marbled, and the glasses were shining more than the sun itself. Manoj wore his black unsuiting sunglasses but took them off when he entered. They all were eagerly waiting for food. They ordered a pizza, four burgers, and a chicken roll with *laal chatni*. It seemed that the man loved *chatni*.

After some time, the waiter came up with the food. When he was ready to put the plates down, the silent man threw the plate harshly away. The food was spoiled and splattered. Everyone was looking towards them with surprise.

"What the hell, Sharma?" shouted the man loudly. The driver had his eyes open.

"Can't you really see he had brought mutton!" said the silent man loudly again.

"So does it really matter?" asked the man.

"Yes, it does. We don't eat it," replied the cold man.

"I also don't eat meat, but this is not a way to behave or show others," said the man, but he wouldn't listen.

"You don't talk to me like that…"

"What the hell, you ordering me, huh! Listen here, you need to learn manners," warned the man.

"I will show them myself!" he said arrogantly.

Nevertheless, without saying anything, the man stood up. He first cleaned his clothes with his hands and then came near the waiter. He was a small boy. He might be very poor and had mistakenly brought others food.

"Who the hell do you see me as?" asked the man harshly.

"Sir, you cannot talk to me like this," said the innocent boy.

"Who the hell are you?"

Suddenly, the man interrupted him and said, "Hey, don't dare to talk like this."

"Remain silent," he replied sharply, and the man was amazed.

"Hey! Do you listen to me, you piece of shit!" said the man with more anger.

"Why do you just bark like this?" said the driver, but the man showed him to be silent.

"You are nothing but a piece of shit, you inferior shit!"

Everyone was watching them, and even some were making videos, but the assistant told them to stop.

"Hey, please don't take him seriously," said the assistant to the waiter, who seemed to be a patient person.

"Yes, sir…"

Suddenly, another man slapped the waiter very hard, and he fell to the ground. Everyone was watching and surprised.

"We don't need…"

SHOT! Suddenly, there was a sudden gunshot. Everyone shouted loudly and rushed here and there. The food sprinkled everywhere and there was no space. The police were around them but watching silently. This was the most horrific scene for the public there. A man was shot dead in front of everyone. There was much squealing and shouting.

"SILENCE!" shouted the man. Everyone was silent and still. The people were astounded; they were out of their reaction time and senses.

He had the gun, blood on his hands, and a man was lying dead on the chair. His face looked fierce. His beard was fully black, and his eyes seemed like a warning zone. He put his leg on the table, the gun in his hand with the support of his knee.

"India is a democratic country," he said and prepared to leave. Everyone had their mouths open and could not understand anything. The waiter was silent but proud of the man. He seemed horrified but inside he was praising the man.

The people went crazy. The police had warned them not to open their mouths. If someone was found doing so…

The police took the body, and what they did to it, they know, and God knows.

He showed Manoj his finger, and they all left to the car. They had forces with them, and everything was in control.

"Sir?" Manoj gulped.

"Hmm,"

"What will we do now?"

The man first looked at him angrily and then replied, "Move to Delhi!"

Manoj could not feel anything after he saw the man lying down. He was numb and did not even blink his eyes. He was in trauma and still could not understand anything.

The man opened the door and sat down on the seat. He started the engine and was ready to leave. He had directed the driver to sit at the back.

❧

When they walk or when they talk, we feel odd.

And when they do good, we simply nod

Whether we like them or not.

The problems around us, we never sort;

We feel above them and never even love them.

We can't feel it every time, but they can be a gem;

Can we ever erase the thoughts that we have taken for granted?

Can we ever give them love they ever wanted;

Should we stop or continue this race of life?

Or just bury them under the power of our knife;

Don't they live like us, or do they have horns?

And when we feel superior, the angel mourns;

We are not greater, or they are lesser than us.

They live, they shine, and they roam like us.

❧

The man was feeling fresh. The car was moving. His shirt was red, and he had cleaned his face. The driver at the back was still silent and did not even give a reaction. Manoj was feeling a burden on his heart. He was sometimes looking at the man, the road, or the sky, everywhere at intervals of time. The man was initially driving somewhat slowly. However, after some time, they were in a tunnel and the speed was over 140. The driver was going crazy and could not even breathe, and Manoj was just watching the road ahead. His body was moving left and right with the turns of the car, but he rarely gave any reaction.

"He was worth nothing!" said the man.

"Sir, what is your name?" said Manoj without looking at him, but his vision was constantly towards the road.

The man sighed and said, "What can it be?"

"Your name is Vikram Rathore,"

The man smiled and said, "Who the hell is he now?"

"Then I don't think you are a real IAS officer,"

"It took me three years to crack the UPSC, and you are now making fun of my misery!"

"But the way…"

"Stop this nonsense talk and say something about yourself," suggested the man, who seemed calm now.

The driver sighed and patted his own head hard. He looked back and saw tons of cars following them. He closed his eyes and bent back in the seat. Not everything was normal. He seemed to know something about the man that others didn't.

Suddenly, the bloody man got a phone call. He saw it was Sharma Banaras. He accepted the call.

"Hello," said the man.

"HELLO," cried the man on the phone.

"What happened?" the man asked with curiosity, thinking that he was captured. "Why are you…"

"What the hell! Did you kill a man just now?" he asked tensely.

"You have a big party giving you news!"

"What the hell, man. I don't care whether you kill someone or bury anyone, my money should be safe!"

"You are again?"

"Oh! Sharma, Karan Sharma from Banaras. I know you, man. Don't act strange. Please don't tell him anything."

"Hmm," replied the man arrogantly.

"Keep it safe and return soon as I have much work for you."

"Oh! Yes, it will be safe. What was the account again?"

"Please don't be loose right now, I want my 200 crores safe!"

"My goodness," the man replied with a huge sigh, "900 crores!"

"Don't yell and what!" shouted the man from the other side.

"Come on, man, I am joking, relax!" he smiled from his side.

He hung up the phone and continued with Manoj, who pretended that he didn't hear anything.

"Sir, why don't you tell me?" asked Manoj in gloom.

"Now what do you want to listen?"

"Who are you?" he asked again with some anger.

"I am no one," said the man and smiled.

"Sir, why don't you trust me?" he was surely fed up.

The man looked in the mirror and saw the driver nodding his head. The driver was bald but was quite cunning.

"What do you want to seek?" asked the man with hope of getting a desirable answer, but he got something troublesome to interpret.

"You," said Manoj hopefully, "*You*, real you!"

The man closed his eyes and heard a scream and someone pushing the handle! When he opened his eyes, suddenly they got hit by a truck, a *barachakki*.

Some people took them to a hospital immediately. Their condition was very serious, except for the driver. He was in a safe zone. The man was in bed, and Manoj was in ICU. The man was unconscious. He suddenly opened his eyes. He was harshly moving here and there. A nurse came to him.

"Doctor!" she screamed, "Doctor!"

There was a hustle there. The doctors came and checked him. He had a heart attack and was shifted to an operating room. He was very serious and had to go through surgery.

After some hours, there was a call. It was incoming to the hospital.

"Hello," said the nurse. "It is …"

"I don't care who you are," said someone harshly. "Where is he?"

"Excuse me, who are you?"

"Tell me, where is he?"

The nurse was silent as she checked the line. She was shocked. It was from the office of the *Prime Minister*.

"Sir…"

There was silence, and the man seemed to be very irritated.

"Hello!" he shouted loudly. The nurse was nervous.

"Yes, sir," she said and breathed heavily. "Who are you looking for?"

"VIKRAM RATHORE!"

"Sorry, sir, we don't have any patient named Vikram Rathore,"

"Shut the fuck up!" he shouted from the side enough to make the innocent girl tremble.

"What sir?" she asked in reflex.

"A criminal never uses his real name!" said the man from that side.

"Which criminal?" asked the scared and confused nurse.

"We are coming there as soon as possible and keep the man with you."

Suddenly, the line was cut. She tried to call them back, but it was not possible.

She was confused and went to the heads for further inquiry. They checked everyone who was there. However, the man was in ICU and was not ready to inquire because he was suffering. The doctors were upset because of his condition.

Someone needed to be there with him. Death could take him anytime. They inquired about the man's belongings. The police searched with the help of the IT team and found a number. It belonged to a girl; they identified her by the photo on it. The name was written as TMCGE. They called her immediately.

⁓

She reached within no time, and with her was an old man. He had a long white beard and *topi* on his head. They rushed in harshly. The girl, after seeing him, was almost going to faint. She sat near him and cried as much as she could. She was crying and crying and kissing his hand badly.

Nevertheless, the old man did not interrupt them and was sitting on a chair, looking at him constantly.

Manoj recovered. He was still unfit but was able to move and talk. He went mad after seeing the man's condition.

"What happened to him?" he asked everyone like a mad kid. He was moving here and there, looking at him for a glance and then watching the old man.

"Who are you now?"

"I am Abdul Majid," replied the man softly.

"I don't care whether you are the PM or the president," he said rudely. "What happened to him?"

"Son, I don't know," he said in a very calm voice. "I told him that you should not leave this time, the police…"

The man squeezed his hands and shouted as hard as he could. He was irritated by everything and the incomplete sentence.

"What happened?" said the old chap calmly.

"I want to know who he was," he cried, and then sat down near the old man's feet.

"He was and is a humble man, son," he replied with pride.

"No, I want to know, really…" he cleared his throat. "I know that you know everything. He is someone I see as very special, please tell me, sir!"

"Son, I am his old uncle, how come I will know about him," he said and seemed not much cautious.

"Who is she, crying?" Manoj asked while pointing to the girl.

"His beloved one!" replied the old man confidently.

"What beloved?"

"Son, listen, I know you must be fascinated by him for nothing!" he said in vain.

The other man was watching him warily, but the old man smiled and continued.

"Think about why you want to know about him. There is no answer!"

"He is special, extra special," replied Manoj with a beacon of hope.

"Why? Any answers?" questioned the man to silence him.

The other man was silent and did not say anything. They were talking when someone called them out.

"Sir, please take that lady with you and come to reception," said a nurse who wanted them to follow her through the corridor to the reception. She had lank hair.

The two men were ready, but the girl was not ready to leave the hands of the lying man.

"Sir, please, I request you to take her with you,"

After many tries, the old man convinced her. They walked slowly through the corridor and reached the reception.

There was an old woman at the reception with short and curly hair. She had some basic spectacles on.

"So, ah…"

"Ma'am, I bought them,"

"Yes, I see you can go now!"

The other nurse went without saying anything. The old nurse lifted her eyebrow and talked.

"So, what's the name of the patient?" she pointed to the girl, but she was only crying, so the old man was ready to answer.

He cleared his throat and said with hesitation, "Mr. Varun Mehta."

The nurse smiled and asked, "Profession?" with extra effort on the word.

The old man again cleared his throat and replied, "He is currently a collector."

"From where?" she inquired oddly.

"Not yet posted but ready to…"

"What about this lady down?" she interrupted him.

The man could not understand anything at first, but then remarked, "Oh!" and said, "She is his…"

But he couldn't continue.

"Wife…"

"Ah! No," he was not ready to answer.

She asked them to leave for the waiting room.

"Why?" cried the lady, crying.

"He is having an operation, so you may wait," she replied stiffly and firmly.

❧

The old man took her with him silently and sat on a chair. The lady was crying very hard, but the old nurse was not even giving a care!

The old man was watching the nurse, but he remained silent. He knew something was not normal here. They waited for much time. A man passed in front of them carrying a kiosk of newspapers.

There was a major headline visible: "INDIA: DEMOCRATISED TO DEMARCATED!" The old man smiled. He looked kind of satisfied and looked at the girl and put his hand on her head and prayed to God for good. There even was a painting hanging on the wall. It was of a dell with 'Don't worry for now or later, just don't worry' written. There were other paintings too, of mickey mouse, probably for children.

They were there for a long time, but no one came and asked them anything. There was not much hustle in the hospital, as if they had prohibited people from coming there.

But after a few hours, someone came there and began to talk.

"Are you with Mr. Varun?"

"Yes," replied the old man.

"Sorry, but he is no more!"

PART 2

2

The Birth of Legend

Life is ephemeral. It is temporary. It is of a short purpose. The earth originated billions of years ago, and you live for only some time here on rent. However, what you do here remains for centuries, if you want. Some people tried and try and will try. Some succeed, and some get busted. This tale is of a legend whose short purpose was for truth, dark reality, conventions, myths, stereotypes, hope, and more importantly: "what no one ever tried"

It was a dark, rainy night in a very big hospital. A woman was on the bed crying of labor pain. There were three doctors who were assigned to her. They were expecting a c-section, but the delivery was normal without any surgery. They were providing all the necessities, and after some time, there was a loud cry of a baby. The husband of the woman was outside. When he heard it, he was full of tears. It was his child.

"Congrats Mr. Rathore, it is a man," said the doctor and laughed. His mother was watching his feet. He was just born yet he scratched his left leg with his right one like an adult, and this made the woman smile. The boy cried a lot, but when he went to his father, he remained silent. There was no fatuity that the boy was rude. His father made him wear a gaudy silver chain on his wrist.

It was adjustable. Even a big person could wear it. It looked bulky on him but showed some royalty. The gore blood of the woman was on the bed, and some house workers cleaned it later. It was a moment of happiness. The man called his father, the child's grandfather.

"Hello, *papa!*" said the man with excitement.

"Goodness, is it a boy?" he replied tensely.

"YES!" said the boy's father happily.

The old man was laughing happily and just was not responding. He seemed to be in heaven.

The voice was fading from the old man's side.

"Listen, it is a boy…" he was telling everyone, and the man was laughing from here but thought, 'What if it was a girl?'

Suddenly, the woman said, "Hey, listen, give him here,"

He smiled and gave him to her. He was adorable, and his mother was full of tears.

"What should we name him?" she said. "Something brave, victorious, and full of courage!"

His father smiled and replied, "Vikram!"

"My Vikram!" responded the woman sweetly and kissed the boy on his forehead. It was 11th of May, and it was his birth at night. He was born at sharp 11 pm. His father celebrated his birth and distributed sweets to all people in the hospital. Everyone was happy with the birth of Vikram. He had a strong face and a strong body. However, the most important thing was: was his mind strong?!

They slept peacefully, but his mother could not. She was thinking of him, how he would be. She would love him until death. Meanwhile, he was sleeping happily and making odd faces. She liked the name Vikram and wished that this boy should be renowned everywhere and he must do some great work.

At home, grandfather was waiting for him. More eagerly, his grandmother, uncles, aunts, and cousins were waiting. All were so excited to see him. They had prepared and decorated the house. The house was made of old style. It was large. They called it *kothi*.

There were lights all around, and neighbours were waiting for him. They were excited for his name. They did not know his name because it was to be revealed the next day. The night passed peacefully.

Next day, all were ready to see the gem of the family. The car arrived, and the women were ready with plates containing all the needed accessories and things, like *diya*, flowers, and *kaala teeka*. When they stepped outside, everyone was surprised to see the boy. He was handsome and cute; the first is quite odd for a newborn, but he was just like his father.

However, his looks were fierce. He looked very active and sensitive. Everyone came and kissed him, blessed him, praised him. Some gave money, which his mother took after refusing, but others insisted very hard. After all the formalities, they came in. Vikram's mother rested on a bed and they served her with good food. They all enjoyed. Vikram remained with his grandfather that day the most. They were Punjabi but lived in UP. They had shifted due to financial problems. They lived just like Punjabis. The house, dressing, food and all the other things were the same as in Punjab. The vibe did not get old. The house, dressing, food and all the other things were the same as in Punjab. *The vibe did not get old.*

Vikram was getting the most love he could. However, the family he had was very primitive-thinking type, stereotypic, and had normal superstitious vibes all around.

Vikram was now six months old. He was very cute, and everyone wanted to make him sit in his or her lap. Unfortunately, the other members did not get a pleasant experience while holding him, he only felt comfort in his father's, mother's, and his grandparents' laps. He remained with his grandfather most of the time. Everyone thought that he would be like his grandfather, Balbir Singh, but no one was aware that he was going to be his toughest ever opponent.

'To whom who love more, you question them more, and with whom you have hatred, you love them more.' It might not suit here. However, everyone lives this way, even if he or she is not even aware of it. A truth that is not realised.

He was not aware of anything other than milk and some love he was getting. He was very young to know about society, but when he gets to know, he might not be like other kids.

"Just like his *dada!*" everyone used to say.

His grandfather adored him a lot. They all adored him. Once a kid in their family had unintentionally made the baby cry. He had to be in great remorse because his grandfather had slapped him and not given food for 2 days. His mother told, exaggerating the fact that he was just not given a sweet that everyone else got.

He was slowly turning a year. Everyone had thought of their gifts. The family had a grandfather, grandmother, their two sons, and three daughters. Their first son was Mohan Singh, who had three children: two sons and one daughter. The second was Rathore Singh, father of Vikram. Vikram had an elder brother. The first daughter was Mohini, she had three sons; the second was Sarita, she had one son and one daughter. The third was Prerna, she had only one daughter.

Vikram's brother loved him very much. His name was Vijay. He used to make Vikram sit on his lap, usually watered by Vikram. He was very fond of his little brother. He believed that he would raise him to be naughty.

It was now time for Vikram's first-year birthday ceremony. The family had invited many relatives to the function. A photographer was also invited. The grandfather had initially declined because he had once exasperated him for no reason. They somehow convinced him to allow the man.

The house was shining like an ornament. The lights had surrounded the house. It was looking like a royal *mahal,* palace. All were ready with gifts.

"Where the hell is that bastard?" shouted grandfather with anger.

His daughter, Mohini, was there, listening.

"Papaji, what are you saying? Everyone is listening," she said with a very serious mood.

"What is everyone doing! That *behenchod* is busy for nothing."

"Shut up, Papaji!" she replied harshly. She went inside and started to look for the photographer. Finally, she found him.

"Ho, *Bhaiya!*" she pointed to the photographer. He was quite young but had no beard.

"Yes," he replied while setting his camera.

"Can you please report to Papaji?" she told him innocently.

"Why?" he replied quickly as if he also didn't adore him.

"I don't know, he just…"

"OK, OK, I will just go," he replied quickly and went with the camera in his hand.

"So mulish!" he thought to himself and found the old man. He hated him more than the old man hated him. They had a bit of an argument in the past, on the lighting of his photo.

"Yes, sir, you called me?" he asked respectfully.

"Oh! You are the bas… I mean the photographer," he said with a grin. "I wanted a photo of myself."

"Yes, of course!" he said with disgust. "Please come here, near the lights."

The old man did so and gave a daring pose, rounding his moustache. He said, "I should look like a king!"

"Yes, sure!" the man replied. "Look like a king, the despotic, uncivilised and a foolish one," he thought to himself again. He did not seem to have the guts to talk straightforwardly to one's face.

The old man was looking for the little prince. He wanted to be the first one with him to take photos.

They had invited many people. For the arrangements, they had hired many workers. Some for cooking, some for lights, some for serving, and so on.

A worker was walking by when a so-called elite-class person crashed into him. His shoes were buried in sauces, along with his pants. He was irate. He wanted to beat him.

"Oh! You little son of a bitch!" he shouted and pushed the man aside. He was feeling very insulted. He was almost ready to beat him when Vikram's mother came there. She handled everything.

"What happened?" she shouted very loudly.

"This son of a brat just…" he came forward to push him again but was stopped by the lady.

"What are you doing? It wasn't his mistake," she said as she really was seeing there at that time. "You crashed with him!"

"Shut up…"

Suddenly, the lady slapped him hard.

"You are rich, that doesn't mean you are everything!" she said very naturally but with a bit of anger.

"How you slapped me!" he replied and was ready to slap her. His hand was in mid-air when it was stopped by her husband.

"Stop and leave," he said very calmly.

"You think you are everything. They are humans and morally better than you," said the lady and looked towards the worker who was feeling humiliated.

Finally, the old man came and joined in.

"What happened? Why are you shouting?" said the old man in surprise.

"This man crashed into him, and in return, he himself started to show himself…"

"Ok! Ok! Stop it all," interrupted her husband, Mr. Rathore.

The man who pushed the worker had left while cursing them all.

"May God ruin your bastard family. May hell be your destiny!" He shouted very hard along with some other words.

While hearing his words, the men in the family were enraged.

A relative, young adolescent, with a long beard and a black *pagdi*, went inside quickly but fiercely and bought a double-barrel shotgun. He was stopped by dozens of people and then, after some time, he relaxed.

"Ho! That bastard was looking at my dada with his bare eyes," he said. "I will snatch his eyes!"

Everything was normal then. After all, they were Punjabi. They all went on to celebrate.

❧

Who are you? Are you an alien, a robot, or a human like me?

Who are you? Are you good, better, or best as you see;

Life is not the same and never can be for me or you,

If no one is listening to you and still saying you are who?

I am the best, better, or good, whatever you want,

But if you think I am your puppet, then I am not;

I am a worker or I am a learner; I can be anyone here.

You tell me who you are if you are barking from there;

I can be a teacher, police officer, or army personnel, or I can even be a leader,

I can even be a babysitter, if your tasks for me need a feeder;

I was, from birth till my last breath, a king,

I may be a singer who can just sing;

I am a labourer or a provider or setter as per my wish,

I can be the king of the jungle or just as small as a fish;

I am someone that I wanted to be.

If you want me to do it, you can see;

Live your life with joy and fun and never let yourself down like a kid,

You don't have to be a loser or someone who hides like he hid;

The celebrations began. Everyone was happy. The songs were playing on speakers. Everyone was first drinking and eating some delicious meals. There was a buffet of chicken, meat, champagne, beer, juices, korma, salad, chocolates and *barfi, laddoo, soan papdi, Pani Puri* stalls were there. Everyone at least visited it ten times.

They all were dancing, and the best dancer was the old man. They were enjoying. Vikram was standing and trying to balance himself in his mother's hands, which he failed to do. After some time, she was behind him and moving his hands to make him dance. She then gave him a small piece of cake. He enjoyed the vanilla most.

&

"Can I get a cup of tea, daughter?" pleaded the old man to Vikram's mother.

"Yes, of course, Papaji!" she replied and gave Vikram his hands. Their house was very large. It was glowing in the city. Big personalities came there, invited by Vikram's father.

Vikram was looking forward to his mom. He was on stage. His grandfather was holding him. At that time, he actually spoke his first word: 'Ma-ma'.

His grandfather was about to cry. He was amazed. Then he just cried aloud. "Listen, everyone, on this beautiful occasion; Vikram Rathore has spoken his first words!"

His mother also heard it and was really happy and excited at the same time to hear his first word. No one knew what the word was except the old man, and he was going to announce it.

"He just said the word, and I really can't hold myself up!"

"Papaji, what did he say?" asked his youngest daughter, Prerna, quickly.

"He just said 'dada'!"

Everyone was applauding hard, and his mother was really happy. He hadn't talked for almost a year. Now, when he talked, his mother was relieved.

It was now time to cut the cake. Everyone was excited, and they all went to a very large hall inside the house. They were eager to see the cake-cutting. But by that time, some people had already left, and no one cared.

"Listen everyone!" announced the old man. "We are today celebrating the first birthday of Mr. Vikram Rathore, as you know," he cleared his throat, "so now we are going for the cake-cutting ceremony."

His mother held his hands, and then he started cutting the cake. Everyone was saying, "Happy Birthday to you, happy birthday to you, happy birthday, dear Vikram, happy birthday to you!"

Meanwhile, he himself was touching the cake and then tasting it, which made some of them laugh. He was finally a year old. He was looking fantastic. His hair was pitch black, and his eyes were light brown, which looked very different; they were hazel to be more specific. He was very handsome, just like his father.

They celebrated for a very long time. They all slept at around 3 or 4 a.m. They were really tired but it was worth it. They spent the day so happily. Though, no one even remembered the fight with the man. It was normal for them. Maybe Vikram might grow up with fights. He will obviously learn from his parents and the family members. And what he probably could learn was love and violence.

Next day, his mother was making him say the word "dada," but he wasn't saying it at all. She tried her best. She was really surprised when he actually said, "Mama."

"You listened!" she pointed to a woman nearby. She nodded her head. It might have meant nothing for that woman, but it was one of the happiest moments of Vikram's mother.

She announced it everywhere. Everyone was normal except the old man; he looked tense and kind of red.

"I might have…"

"No problem, Papaji, it happens!"

"No, no, he really said 'dada' and now he won't. He may be shy right now."

"No matter, Papaji, congratulate Vikram."

The old man was feeling angry and embarrassed as well. He took Vikram in his lap and muttered something in his ears. "Why couldn't you be silent, you filthy kid?"

The kid was making a rustling, funny noise after hearing the old man.

"I guess it is his milk time," said his mother and took him from the old man's lap, and took him to another room.

She was elegant. She believed in equality. She empowered the so-called inferiors and declined discrimination and hate. She was morally great and she was truthful. She taught others goodness and herself followed the same path. She was Maria. She was from Karnataka, Bangalore. She was quite modern but did not follow the usual modern path. She wore traditional dresses and believed truly in God. She taught Vijay the good things and was eager to teach Vikram as well.

She believed that she was going to be his first teacher and the best one ever. She believed that Vikram would choose peace. Even though she behaved very well and was more disciplined than anyone else, she was not much preferred in the family. The reason was something that was hidden from everyone. She was like the normal ones but truly the best. She was a computer engineer herself but she chose to work at home and help others.

Vijay's father remained out most of the time, so she had to fend for him. She took really good care of him. She taught him school work and gave him extra knowledge. He was considered the best and brightest student in class, only because of his mother.

It was now Vikram's turn to be the best. But what could he be best at? The best in peace, the best in studies, or the best in fighting!

He was learning at his own pace. He might have been around one and a half years old when he had learned to say the letter 'a'. He spoke many words like 'mama', 'dada' (at least the old man was happy!), 'papa', 'nana', 'Gandhi ji', 'sir', and obviously 'a'.

He was getting cuter but still full of rage. His toddling period was kind of odd. He used to run here and there. He was very quick and swift. He even once said to a boy, who teased him for a joke, 'I am gonna maim you and send you to hell, you son of a brat!'

⋙

He seemed curious about everything. No one knew how much more inquisitive he would be in the future.

3

The Unusual Boy

The little kid was now two years old. He was now a perfectly normal family member. No one actually cared much about him after some time. He had become a normal person of the family. He was now a toddler. He had an odd grin. He had two teeth on the upper jaw and two on the mandible. But he had spaces between them. He was acting just like a kid should, but his rage was outspoken. He used to get angry at everything. If someone stranger touched him, he used to give a high-pitched cry, which made others close their ears. He hit them and used his nails to scratch them or even bite their hands.

His family members didn't mind much because they were used to him. He was normal if he shouted, or if he cried, or even if he fainted, not himself but others. He seemed to be scared of nothing but cotton. Whenever he saw some cotton, it was the only time he cried for himself. He was naughty. He sometimes went to power supply areas which were dangerous, so to avoid it, the wires were covered with cotton which freaked him. He then never ever went there.

He didn't walk until he was 2. When he was almost one and a half years old, he first time moved, using his legs and hands. They recorded him while that moment using a camera, alas! No cameraperson was there. The old man wished that a photographer were there; so that he could do some warm-up on him.

The first time he got up using a bed and using his legs only to move, or just he walked like any other in the family, it was the most delightful moment. He was a late walker, maybe, for the family. No one knew if he was going to be a late talker, a late learner, or a late whatever. He didn't give a shit. He was enjoying his own world. Whenever he heard some music, he danced on his own and moved his head here and there. He was himself and didn't care about anyone.

He could not talk much. His agers were talking fluently but he was able to speak only some selected words or phrases. He seemed to be silent most of the time. His grandmother said, "He is just like his father, more action, less talk only actions." And laughed.

Everyone else agreed and didn't mind. But his father felt rather odd when he heard this. That family was elegant and loving. They were not involved in crimes anyway.

❧

The riots were common in those days, but they never joined as they thought it was just a waste of time. Why can't people live with harmony?

But the old man seemed to be indulgent. He hated others but did not show it to his family. He wanted to kill the other religious people and Muslims. But in turn, his son, Rathore Singh, actually preferred peace. He did not hate anyone but he used to eat and enjoy with others, whether they be Muslims or Hindus. He believed that everyone should live in fraternity and we are all brothers and sisters. The words hate and kill were normal for the others and the old man but not for the remaining family. Vijay, who knew nothing of riots, usually avoided even thinking about them.

His mother, as per her nature and character, taught him the merits of every religion. She was a true scholar and philosopher, not like those like Kiran Mehta Singh. He was the leader of a private party called 'Hail Hindu' and he promoted killing Muslims. However, they were not alone in their actions, as Abdul Majid, the leader of the 'Muslim Rise Party', was also involved in killing many Hindus. They were each other's bloodiest enemies.

Meanwhile, Vikram's family only knew fun, enjoyment, and food. The family was fond of eating. They usually made new feasts and enjoyed them. Not only did they enjoy, but they also sent a large part of the food to neighbours. They were respected in the area. Everyone loved them, and they loved everyone else, excluding the old man, of course.

The donations were common in the family. They went to Gurudwaras and donated food and clothes. Vikram's father knew a man and gave him food and clothes to donate in Masjids. And one more friend also donated in temples.

They believed that the more you share, the more you prosper. Vikram also learned some lessons from his family. He was also fond of doing what others did. But one more quality of his was brutality. He did not spare anyone. He liked it when someone was being beaten or when some kids fought in the colony. Even though he was just three years old, he liked crimes more than a criminal did.

When he was three years old, he went to a mosque. When he came back, the old man was on fire.

"Where the hell were you!" he barked.

"For praying," he replied smoothly, "you told me to!"

"To a Masjid? I said to a Masjid!" he replied harshly.

"No, but you said praying," he said very calmly.

"So go to the Gurudwara!" said the old man with his moustache on his head.

"But what matters is praying!" replied the young boy with essence of leadership.

"WHAT?" the man said firmly, in anger.

"Yes! You told me to pray. I prayed to God. No one said that God has only one place. God is everywhere, he knows what we want and still there was a large crowd in Gurudwara!"

"There was donating *halwa!*" added his father smoothly.

Once, he went with Vijay to the playground. He was three years old, maybe more than that but less than four years old. They were walking when they were facing a dog face to face. The only thought that came to the mind of Vijay was whether they could escape, but the thought that emerged within Vikram was from where they could beat him harder.

The dog's mouth was open, growling, and saliva was pouring down slowly.

Vijay muttered to Vikram, "Brother, don't run or he will jump on us and we will be left with nothing!"

Vikram in turn replied coolly, "Brother, we should get past the dog and hit him with a stone, so that he could not escape"

Vijay was out of his wits. He shook his head resentfully. But little did he know that Vikram's hand was already full of pebbles. In no time, he went forward and hit the pebbles as hard as he could and ran toward the dog. Vijay's eyeballs were already out, and he fiercely ran after him. He thought he had lost a brother and had to wait for another one.

The dog had mutilated Vikram's hand. Instead of crying, he breathed hard on the wound and kicked the dog in the face. The dog, in turn, was crying hard, and Vikram was jerking his hand painfully yet calmly.

"We shall hit you with a musket!" shouted the old man at Vijay. He was speechless as he could not make it clear that Vikram had been harmed, and he was not crying, but the dog was instead crying. He tried to say it first but got slapped by his father. His only thought was, "bust elder brothers, why am I older!"

He then didn't talk with Vikram for some time. "Bhaiya! Come, let's go to the playground," he said, but Vijay was looking fiercely towards him and shook his head.

"Show some consideration for your brother, Vijay," said his mom, "You are so rude!"

But what could he reply!

"Obligation!" he shouted. "I understand, but to him for what? He is a nonsense little boy full of dummy brain and nothing!"

"Shut up?" replied his mom, and he remained silent for a long time.

Then he was ordered to take his brother to school for one day. He was out of his mind.

"SCHOOL? HIM? ME?" he shouted.

"Are you mad? What are you muttering?" said his father.

"I ain't doing it!" he replied and was ready to jump in a well instead of doing that action.

"Remember," said his mom, and he had no other choice. His brother was fully ready. His reason for not taking him to school was not the previous one but something else he did not want Vikram to know!

He got ready, wore his uniform, and had his lunch, whereas Vikram was already outside waiting for the bus.

"Come inside, nuts! The bus ain't coming for you this soon!" he shouted when the bus just arrived. He was red like an apple and left without saying anything. His mother smiled, touched his head, and he was ready to leave. He was looking in the garden when Vikram whistled through the window!

"That little brat!" he thought in his mind because he couldn't shout at that time for many reasons.

He quickly ran towards the bus and went in. He waved to his mother and the bus left. He found a seat and sat there. He looked for the little boy when he was shocked. He was sitting on a seat where he was surrounded by girls from all sides. This was the first time Vijay got to know what jealousy actually meant.

"Hey!" he shouted to Vikram who was enjoying his ride, "Come here, sit with me."

"Wait a minute!" he replied to his brother coolly. "Who are you?"

After hearing this, Vijay was helpless as the girls laughed at him. He wanted to go and slap his brother. He was envious.

"So, what do you like?" Vijay heard some girl muttering this to Vikram who was replying in no time. He was really cute; Vijay had to admit, but this much of attraction! Honey surrounded by bees. "I never was surrounded by ladies when I was little," he thought to himself.

The bus was moving swiftly and they were near to school. Just ten minutes and they would reach there. "Tihar Jail," some students quoted on school, but Vijay was normal and didn't even think anything about school. There was something else about school that he always thought about.

It was a secret, obviously, and he could not remain normal when he thought about it. Meanwhile, they could see the school. It was large, five stories high, yellow and white coloured, enormous, and beautiful. But who cared? It was normal for them but not for the little naughty boy. He thought of many things to do in school, which only he knew, and grinned to himself.

When everyone was exiting the bus, Vijay saw Vikram with really mean eyes. He stiffly held his hand and pushed him hard, only until a madam came in front of him.

"Good morning, ma'am!"

"Good morning, Vijay!"

"How are you, ma'am?"

"Fine, *beta*!" said the teacher happily. "Who is this cutie?"

He stood still, coldly, and replied unintentionally, "My brother."

"Oh! He is so cute. How are you, mister? Oh, fine, so cute!"

"Ma'am, can I go now?" he asked meanly.

"Of course, *Beta*, go," she said, but was constantly looking at Vikram with adorable eyes and regretted later because she forgot to ask his name.

They were walking through the corridor and the same thing happened. Every teacher was asking about him. Vijay found it irksome. He was amazed to see that today all the girls were present in the class, *that day!*

When he just entered the class, everyone was looking at him and then at the little boy. They were shocked. Some of his friends knew he had a brother, but this little boy, they hadn't expected.

"Hey, Vijay!" said a boy, surprisingly, "Don't tell me he's your brother!"

He was so irritated that he didn't even reply; instead, he sat on the chair and opened his books.

"Tell me *na!*" he insisted.

"What?" asked Vijay as if he didn't hear.

"Is he your brother?" guessed the boy.

"What do you expect from me?" he said when he was finally tired of everything. "Shall I bring a model or an actor's newborn rich baby here to show you?"

"No, I didn't say he is a model, but…"

"Yeah, don't expect me to come with a beggar baby!" he said and sighed in anger.

Vikram was full of rage when he heard this.

"Brother!" he pointed to the other boy who was talking. "You also don't expect me to come with a beggar himself!"

No one could stop his laughter. Vijay was out of his mind. He hit Vikram on the back of his head and directed him to sit next to him quickly.

To Vijay's surprise, all the girls were looking at him. He thought, "What is so special about his brother?" But then he dismissed the thought and ignored everyone.

Then it was the time for the first class. The teacher came in suddenly. No one greeted at first, but because of his ferocious look, everyone stood up, including Vikram, and greeted him.

"Good morning, sir," some said gloomily.

But some shouted out energetically, "Konichiwa," which made everyone laugh.

"Sit down, rascals!"

He looked at the class. He didn't notice Vikram at first.

"Open page number sixty-nine," his voice was heavy.

Everyone did so but with a sigh. Some giggled, and Vikram also joined for no reason. It was an English class. Vijay was in 8th grade.

"Wait a minute!" he said with a different energy that he casually had. "Who is that little boy?"

"Vijay's brother," shouted some boy, which made Vijay very angry.

"Oh well! Well, I see something similar, *maybe*," he said with more emphasis on the last word. He somehow tried to stigmatise Vijay for an unknown reason.

"What do you mean by MAYBE?" shouted the almost four-year-old. "Brothers are alike and not only alike but one! No one will say your brother seems like you, MAYBE!"

Without saying anything else, the man continued, "How do you know about my brother?"

"Vikalp Sharma!" replied Vikram, who should not know this. He had died in a communal riot.

"WHAT THE HELL!" shouted the man. "VIJAY, WHAT DO YOU TEACH HIM?"

Meanwhile, Vijay knew Vikram had said more than enough, but he was so happy and proud when his brother announced his first words. Alike and one!

"Sir, I don't know how he knows…"

"You don't know anything, Vijay!" he announced to make him go red, but Vikram was there.

"Sir, for your satisfaction, my brother can speak fluent English better than you, and that is the point of learning English," he said stiffly.

Vijay meanwhile was confused how this little boy could speak this much. Had he saved it for this time? Still, he was afraid Vikram would shout some vulgar words.

"OH MY GOD!" shouted the man. "See how this family is! Father and son alike!"

"That means you are not like your father, sir!" Now contradicted Vikram enough to trigger the teacher.

Without realising, a big argument had broken out! Vijay was preparing his defence speech, which he knew he had to present before everyone as he was his elder brother.

"YOU GET OUT AND COME WITH ME, VIJAY, AND THAT LITTLE BRAT!"

"Your father is a brat! You nuts!"

Now, nothing was left to say. Vijay had decided to jump from the window, but something stopped him. They went out with teachers' faces red as fire. He knew he had to get expelled! They were walking quickly towards the principal's office. Vijay was pale, but Vikram seemed to have something more to say. Vijay seemed to have forgotten his mother tongue!

The teacher angrily knocked on the door and barged inside quickly with Vijay's hand held in his hand.

"What happened, Vikram?" asked the principal to the teacher.

"Sir, do you expect anything from this useless—?" he pointed to Vijay, who was silent throughout the whole conversation until he was asked to speak.

"What do you mean?" asked the principal nonchalantly. "Sir, *this* little boy just abused me in front of everyone!"

"What?" he said in confusion. "Wait, who's that?"

"His younger brother, don't know the name?"

"Vikram," announced the little boy with confidence. To teacher's surprise, his name matched his.

"What have you done, kid?" asked the shaved man.

"Nothing!" he said confidently. "He said bad things about my family, so I defended myself."

"What a liar!" shouted the teacher. "He just said so much. I have lost my dignity."

"Sir, dignity is not taken over by an argument, but if you do something against what needs to be done!" quoted the little boy, which surprised the principal.

"Ah! Vikram, sir, you leave. I will look into it."

Without wishing, the man had to move outside. When he finally closed the door, the principal continued. To Vijay's surprise, he changed the topic.

"Who told you that, little boy!"

"What?" he replied. "Those bad words?"

"NO! That statement you just gave,"

"My mother," said Vikram proudly.

"Vijay, you never told your mother's biopic," he said.

"Sir, you never told me to," he replied coldly.

"What is her name again?" he asked curiously.

"Maria!" he replied in vain.

"From?" asked the principal and scratched his head in order to help him remember something.

"Bangalore," he replied.

"OH MY GOD!" he said, fascinated. "She was my classmate!"

This statement relieved Vijay.

"Really?" asked Vikram.

"Yes! She was the most thoughtful person I ever met! Where is she now?"

"At home," he said, and was sure that the man should be silent now, but he wasn't.

"She used to call me Chotu Bhaiya!"

Vikram giggled, and the principal himself grinned.

"Only she can teach you such insightful thoughts!"

"Yes, sir," replied Vikram.

They had a really long conversation, and it finally ended, and they were spared from punishment. The principal had made a good reason to save them. He had lied about them and saved them.

Vijay was really relieved. He was safe now, and only because of his beloved brother, Vikram!

4

The Brother's Secret

After the incident, Vijay liked Vikram very much. He was usually not able to speak much; hardly and coldly, but his brother! He was scared of nothing. But the thing he feared most was that his brother was hell abusive and intolerant. He was very much curious about his future; in this tender age, he was so aggressive and abusive, and how will he be in the future. And he got to know really fast.

"Vijay!" someone shouted loudly from the ground.

"What happened?" he replied from the upper floor.

"Your brother!"

He knew he had done something that was far worse than getting expelled from the school. He was going to face severe punishment.

He ran down swiftly and saw something horrible. Vikram was holding a bat full of blood, and another kid was crying, his head full of blood! He knew he had done the scene.

"What the hell, Vikram!" he shouted at him.

"I didn't do it just for fun, he…"

"Just shut up!" he interrupted angrily.

"He abused my mother!" Vikram said in anger.

"SO! You should have gone to some teacher," suggested Vijay in a lower note.

"What will he do? He will curse him and leave him!"

"Oh! You don't understand; you are in big trouble," he said in an emphatic voice and quickly bent to the injured boy. He was bleeding. He held him and gave him support. He took him inside the nurse's room, and the nurse was –

"What the hell!" she exclaimed with shock and fear.

"Ma'am, he got injured," said Vijay.

"This much!" she replied with a scary face and a funny voice.

"He got hit by a bat," Vijay tried to defend Vikram.

"Don't tell me it was Vikram!" she had already guessed the culprit.

Ashamed, Vijay nodded his head sorrowfully. The nurse was full of rage. She quickly went out and shouted to Vikram, who meanwhile was continuing his football match.

"HEY VIKRAM, BRAT!" she shouted in anger.

"YES?" he shouted back, normally and peacefully.

"Come here, you monster!" she said with uneasiness.

"What?" he said with an innocent tone and a normal face.

"You have hit another one; you are not human!"

"You *madarchod*!"

"What the hell! YOU SON OF A BIT…"

"Same reaction was mine, ma'am. I ain't done any crime," he said coldly. "If I am wrong, that means you are also WRONG!" he interrupted and made her understand.

The nurse was silent. She understood at once what the matter was. Silently, she went inside while he got the ball again.

She came in stiffly with Vijay, looking scared.

"You small monster, you abused him!" she pointed to the injured boy.

"Ma'am, but he…"

"Silent, I am going to bandage you and call your parents now!"

The boy thought that now Vikram was gone, but something else dawned on him!

"Let them come and let me tell them your holy words!" she said angrily.

He was silent and ready to get beaten more while Vikram was chilling. He knew he had to get some hands on him, but it hardly mattered.

He was in 5th grade. He had been coming to school for the last few years. He managed to top the class in academics as well as bossing around.

He managed to win every girl's heart. He was cool, smart, fashionable, and a gangster as well. He even tried to beat a ninth grader once, which fortunately was ended by the principal himself.

After that incident, he was warned at home.

"Why are you doing these things, Vikram?" said her mother, exhausted.

"You are a total badass!" said his grandfather proudly yet secretly. In front of everyone, he had said, "Very bad!"

"I am not going to spare you; you are creating total indiscipline," a usual quote by his father.

And then, who can forget the old lady of the old man? She was turning red and furious. It looked like she was ready to leave!

"Oh my God! Oh, what has he done! He could have gotten killed, my lord take me! So embarrassing! Just like my hus…"

But then she stopped and regretted talking. The old man looked furious, and he was ready to kill her. Vikram's father was looking pale, and his eyes were out of their sockets.

"Please let me deal with him!" demanded his mother. She looked the most feared of all. She took him away and did not come down till afternoon.

"Why couldn't you control yourself?" cried his mom in the room alone with him. "Because of you, just you!"

"What did I do?" questioned Vikram unpleasantly.

"WHAT DID YOU DO?" she shouted harshly at him. "I am going to empoison you or myself one day!"

Vikram was silent. He felt cold and didn't say anything. He looked serious, really serious for the first time. His eyebrows were locked hard and he hardly had any emotions on his face.

"EMPOISON!" he shouted coldly, which made his mother tremble for a second.

"WHY WILL YOU EMPOISON ME OR YOU?" he shouted, "JUST EMPOISON THE ONE WHO STARTED IT!"

Now, she was silent. She had hardly anything on her face. She couldn't control herself and slapped him hard.

"GO," she shouted! "GO TO HELL, GO DOWN! NOW!"

He couldn't control himself. He ran as fast as he could. He ran down and then directly out. He was really full of anger, but he didn't want to show it. He then went directly to the ground. Kids were playing there.

"Let me play," he demanded.

"After this game," someone replied softly.

"I SAID, LET ME PLAY!"

They had no other choice. They knew what would happen if they refused.

"Be sure you are both sides,"

He didn't give a response and directly went behind the stumps. He surely was just 7 years old, but he was fire. He, at the same time, was really angry. He was cursing everyone he could think of.

"CATCH IT!" shouted a boy on reflex.

Suddenly the ball left the bat, brushing it behind the batsman. And CATCH!

"HURRAH! Love you, Vicky!" said a boy and hugged him.

He was silent as it was his turn now to play. He had just cleared the best batsman of all.

There was an umpire there, a kid who had been cleared before. He was ready to bust Vikram because of what he had done.

"Now here the bowler comes, he throws the ball and…"

He was awestruck! A big six! It is so impossible to think of a little boy hitting big shots. But he was a boy that everyone talked about, either in sports or academics. He was full of talent and agility. So hitting like this was normal for him.

"No one has seen a larger one than that!" said a boy with surprise.

The team was cheering except for the one who just got out. He was really irritated by it.

His anger was relieved, but he still couldn't forget the scene he just went through.

There was another ball. And a four, two runs, a huge six again, not to mention that the boundary was quite large for some of them, but actually it was very little, so they had a tough game. Then, at last, he was out!

Now was the time of the other team, and he still had to play one more inning as he was playing from both sides as a batsman and a keeper. The team played well at first. They had to make 45 in 4 overs.

They had made 20 and now 2 overs left. The last batsman, Vikram, is on the field, finally!

25 in 12! A ball and four! Now 21 in 11, a huge six! 15 in 10, again a four! 11 in 9, two runs! 9 in 8, a miss! But then a miss again. He had to move to the other side!

9 in 6! And other batsman there, a weak one. 2 misses! 9 in 4! Again a miss! 9 in 3 but finally a single! Now it was all on Vikram. 9 in 2!

He hit a four! Now the most intense part, 5 in 1. The ball came very fast. He closed his eyes and hit his bat randomly. He opened his eyes; the ball was nowhere, but the funniest part, the bat was nowhere! It was at the boundary line, and he had hit a six. They praised him, enjoyed, and even gave him a sip from their juice.

He was really happy after that victory. He was relieved. He went home happily, had dinner, and slept. Then it was another day of school!

He was ready and then he went to the bus as usual. Talked, laughed, and did other things. He had a friend on the bus. He always sat with him. He really was not like Vikram. He was sweet and simple. He was not aggressive and angry like Vikram. Still, after knowing the facts, Vikram made him his friend. He didn't know the reason why he liked him but still always cared for him. They were what we call best friends! No one would have ever thought a person like Vikram would have a friend.

They were travelling and talking when suddenly the bus stopped. WHAM!

"What the hell!"

"What has happened?"

"OUCH!"

These were the random and odd reactions made by the kids and the seniors as well. They were really shocked.

Suddenly, the driver shouted from the front, "The tyre is punctured, maybe by a nail, a really big one actually."

"OH NO!" said a boy gloomily, "We are going to miss P.E. class!"

"Sad for you, boy!" replied Vikram coolly as he also had a physical education class but after the lunch break.

"Shut up, Vikram!" shouted the boy. "You aren't deciding my fate!"

This thing hurt Vikram, but he remained silent and gave an odd smile. No one could understand why he was silent this time.

It took them much time, and finally after thirty whole minutes, they reached school. He quickly went out of the bus and then rushed towards the class quickly with his best friend. He was really fast that time. Finally, half panting, half conscious, he reached the classroom.

He opened the door and said, "May we come in, ma'am?"

"You are late, Vikram and Varun!" said the teacher in anger and with tight eyebrows.

"Ma'am, the bus…"

"Shut up, Vikram!" she shouted sternly. "Stand outside the class, both of you."

Vikram found it best not to argue and to be silent. He put his head down and went outside the class silently. Not only the students, but the teacher herself, was shocked to see him. She was ready to argue and fight with him (as he had made his image like that), but he didn't even give a response.

The class was over, and the teacher came outside.

"What is the matter, Vikram and Varun?" she said, this time in a calm voice.

"Ma'am, the bus was punctured, and we reached late!" said Vikram smoothly and softly.

"OH!" the teacher exclaimed, "Go inside the class quickly and, yes, tell them to show you the homework,"

"Ok, ma'am," said Vikram softly again, and gently he went inside.

It seemed odd to some to see Vikram behaving like this. They were confused and some even asked him why he was not ready to fight with the teacher. But he remained silent.

It was the next class, and the teacher was absent that day. Then a man came there; he was the timetable manager who was short and funny.

"Listen," he said absentmindedly, "because of the request from Miss Sumita, you are allowed to go for P.E. class this time."

He was just finishing when everyone shouted and celebrated the announcement. Everyone was happy but to others' surprise, the noisiest and the most P-E loving boy was silent: Vikram!

They went down, and while on the stairs, they were choosing the teams.

"Vikram will be in our team," argued one boy.

"NO! He will be in ours," argued another one.

In the way they met Sumita ma'am, she was a young lady with an age, maybe around 22 years. She taught them science. She was elegant and loved by everyone.

"Have fun, kids!" she said to them and smiled.

"Thanks, ma'am," replied Vikram softly.

They were finally on the ground. The football was ready. He played football at school and cricket at home in their playground, as there was no one who played football there.

The team was set. He was in the weak team, and the other was very strong. It had their best players. They were small, but their craze was enough.

They started. They didn't have goalposts for little children; they had cones. The distance between the two goals was almost half of the actual ground for football.

Vikram decided to take a free kick first from the centre. He had learned everything from his brother. His brother was also a very good football player.

He shot as hard as he could. The ball was in the air and moving like a bullet. For them, it was fast but really it wasn't much. It passed through the goalkeeper's feet as it moved down in a parabola. It was a simple goal but for some, it was a mark of victory and for some a moment of weeping.

They had scored at first. They were celebrating. Again, the ball was in control of Vikram as their defender stopped the ball and passed it to him. He dribbled very well. He went through all the players, unbalanced; the ball came to his left foot. He was in stress as his left foot was very weak. He kicked with all his might and scored again! The ball went very slowly but with an unusual curve that confused the goalkeeper of the opposition. They were celebrating again. Sumita ma'am, was watching through the window, and she smiled.

They played for some time, the opponent even came near the goalpost and shot. Others felt already that it was a goal except Vikram. Miraculously, the goalkeeper, who was weak and bad at sports, stopped it with his hand. He had closed his eyes and given himself up for the sacrifice. They cheered, and the class was over. Most of the time, they kicked the ball randomly and then threw the ball outside many times.

Vikram, after that, was silent again as others were talking about the match. He felt thirsty. So, he went to the filter with his bottle. He was midway when he heard something. He recognised the voice at first!

"I told you I don't have a mobile phone, why do you call on the landline yesterday?"

"But you said you would get your phone soon!" said the girl in a soft and stern voice.

"Listen! I will surely get it, but don't call if someone else picked it. It was lucky that Vikram told me to answer!"

It was surely his brother talking to a girl in a corner near the nurse's room.

"Okay, I will call you from here. Don't you dare to call!"

Vikram moved around a bit.

"Ok! Bye, love you and meet you at departure time!"

"Love you too!" whispered his brother. Quickly, Vikram went to another empty classroom and then, acting like he knew nothing, he normally came out. But he was out of his wits and surprised to hell.

"Hey, Vikram!" said Vijay with a broken voice.

"I was just passing to get some water,"

"Oh! I also came, I had to meet Arjun, sir!" he said confidently, yet he was gulping.

Vikram left without saying anything. Vijay just hoped that he didn't listen to him, and he also left.

Vikram was in chaos. His brother in 10th grade with a girl of 8th grade, chaos!

He was shaking his head in the way Sumita ma'am, saw him while he was walking straight.

"Good afternoon, ma'am," said some students.

"Good morning, *Beta,*" she replied softly.

"Good morning, ma'am," grinned Vikram.

"Played well, dear!" complimented the teacher to Vikram.

"Oh! Thanks, ma'am!" he said and blushed.

She shook her head, smiled and left. He felt positive.

But the thought again emerged. My mom never taught us to do such things! But him! He is a brat! Why did he date a junior! I don't get it! I should tell… no, no, let me keep it a secret and reveal it at the right time!

Then he went to his classroom and continued to study with elegance, but with that thing in mind. It would have distracted him many times if he didn't control himself.

5

The Rise of Terror

The secret of his brother shook Vikram very much! He was in deep shock. He never imagined it. For others, for seniors, it was normal, but no, it was not for Vikram and his family, especially his mother.

He was always looking at his brother oddly, and Vijay had guessed that it had already dawned on him. But why had he not told anyone yet? Maybe Vijay was just guessing, just guessing!

Vikram always found a way to look after his brother for more such conversations. And that happened, just happened.

He was following Vijay secretly when he found that he met her again at the same place.

"Nice to talk to you yesterday!" said Vijay with a sense of fear and relief as well.

"I also liked it!" she replied enthusiastically.

"I am scared that if Vikram found out, he might tell others," said the feared boy.

"Don't worry about that and see how I am gonna care for him and give him such company that he won't be able to speak about me!" She said with a dangerous confidence.

But Vijay knew about Vikram; he knew he wasn't going to give a shit about anyone. He did whatever he wanted to do.

Vikram left quickly as he knew they were going to end up quickly as well. He ran quickly towards the stairs. But on the way, he went to the library.

"May I come in, sir?" asked Vikram to the librarian, who seemed to be busy working but was shocked to see Vikram!

"You are Vikram! Right!" he said in an exclamation, like the opposition leader seeing the opposition leader visiting his home.

Vikram hesitated and nodded his head in an unordered manner.

"Are you here to play or what?" he asked Vikram with a different tone.

"No, sir, not playing," he replied quickly, which turned the librarian pale. "I was just going through books!"

He seemed to cry. He was out of his wits. Vikram went to the library for reading! Unbelievable, and really, he was acting differently than other days.

He was searching through books when he found a book he wanted. It was a book about discipline and self-control. The writer was Shekhar Joshi. The book was titled: 'How to Train Yourself: Discipline and Self-Control'.

The librarian was going mad. He opened the register. His name was Arjun. He was of medium height and had a good beard.

"Hmm! Vikram Rathore! Book number?" he asked in a normal librarian tone, boring.

"Ah! D-111," he replied after seeing the tag on the book.

"D-111, OK, issued!" he said, surprised. "Read it and write its summary for me."

"Ok sir," he said and went quickly. He went upstairs, and the teacher was already in.

He gently knocked on the door and said, "May I come in, sir?"

The teacher simply nodded his head, and Vikram came inside and sat on his chair near Varun.

He was a social science teacher. He was teaching about education at that time. They were having a healthy discussion.

"Vikram! Stand up," he ordered him as casually as he ordered the brightest student to answer an easy question.

"Yes, sir," he replied with moderate confidence.

"Tell me, in your opinion, what are the things lacking in our education system?" asked the middle-aged teacher.

He thought and finally came up with an answer.

"Sir, there are two things lacking in our education system: one is education, and the other is system!"

Everyone laughed except the teacher.

"Sit down, Vikram!" he said while thinking about something, and he smiled at him.

The class was finally over, and the teacher left with a last look on Vikram's face.

"That was awesome!" said Varun excitedly.

"Thanks!"

It was lunchtime, and Vikram went to the library again. But at that time, someone followed him.

He went inside, and after him was a girl of 4th grade; she also came and sat near Vikram.

"Hi!" she whispered.

"Hi," replied Vikram with much of his attentiveness.

"Ah! Are you Vikram?" she asked as if she was meeting him for the first time.

"Yeah,"

"Actually, I wanted to say something to you!" she said, and kind of blushed and smiled.

"Say it!" he said normally.

"Ah! Will you want to be in a relationship with me!" she said with towers of hope in her eyes.

This was left for Vikram's ears. He went pink but was afraid as well, maybe for the first time. The girl was very beautiful, pretty, smart, and loving. She had proposed to him!

"Ah! Well, let me think!" he replied when he could think of nothing else.

"No worries, dear! Take your time," she said and left without any other word.

He was in deep shock. First, his brother and now him! He was frustrated. He didn't know what to do. He decided to read the book first and then decide.

He went back to class. He was pale. He was scared. He was about to pass out!

"What happened?" asked Varun.

"Nothing," he replied casually.

"Tell me *na*!" demanded Varun with a quintessence of excitement.

Suddenly, a teacher came in. She was Sumita ma'am. Everyone stood up and looked excited. Everyone had a crush on her.

"Good morning, sit down!" she said and moved her hair to the back with a swift movement of her head.

"Thanks, ma'am," was the only reply and it was by Vikram.

"Welcome, dear!"

"What do we have to do today?"

"Earth," replied Vikram enthusiastically.

"Ok!"

They started the lecture when a teacher hopped in suddenly.

"Ma'am, leave quickly, and students, move quickly to the ground!"

"What…"

"Just go!" he replied and went out running! He looked tense, and he was breathing like he had ended up fighting in World War II. But the conditions did not seem too well as the noises began to emerge from outside very fast and with fear.

After some time, everyone was outside. They were directed to move to their buses. Everyone was loaded, and they left. No one knew what was happening!

There was a great hustle and bustle in the buses. Each and everyone was making their own theories. Some said the principal died! Some said that there was an attack in school! And it went just like that.

Vikram was just in confusion about what had happened. It was chaos all around. The teachers themselves had gone mad. What happened? No one knew why!

The buses finally departed, and students were directed not to make much noise or just no noise. They didn't tell them the reason for the early departure. The saddest looked Vijay, and Vikram knew why! He had missed the time to meet his girlfriend, of course, he thought.

The bus was moving really fast, and the driver seemed anxious. He was sweating. No one could understand what was happening until they heard cries. They were frightened to death. Heartbeats were fast. People seemed to run and cry out loud. Some cries were of anger, and some of fear of getting killed! And that is when Vikram understood that the thing he feared the most had started.

They reached home safely. His father was waiting outside. He also seemed tense. They got off and entered the house very quickly. Their father was gulping hard, meanwhile the old man was silent and tapping his feet to the ground. He seemed to be thinking about many things.

"What is happening?" said tense Vijay.

"Go to your room and rest there," replied their father.

"What is it?" he repeated with anger.

But before anyone could answer, Vikram kicked his feet and motioned for him to follow him.

They both went to their room.

"What's the matter?" asked Vijay with his little eyes, "Why is nobody responding?"

"Listen!"

"What?"

"These are the riots!"

"What?" he replied as if he didn't know what the word meant.

"Yes! People are off now. They have started it. They are now not gonna see who is standing. They are now ready for war. No one can do anything! We have to be safe. They are the radicals."

"BUT WHY?"

"They are all sons of bitches! They don't know why they are even doing this. They are fighting, and innocent people are affected. They don't know why they are fighting. They want their own dominance, BUT I DON'T UNDERSTAND WHY! Why they need it!"

"Power!"

"Power is not what you get by fighting and killing, but by winning hearts."

"Don't you try to speak outside or they will kill you!"

"I ain't scared of no bitch!" exclaimed Vikram.

"SHUT UP! Be silent and don't be harsh. Stay calm."

"I don't care and I ain't scared of anyone."

Vijay sighed and patted his brother's shoulder.

"I know you are not scared, but this is how society works, and we also have to work like that."

"HELL NO! I don't care what society does or what they want. I care about myself and my feelings," he said coldly.

Vijay remained silent and didn't reply as he knew Vikram was born different. He wouldn't care about anyone. He would do whatever he wants.

"Ok, I believe you are good, but what are you going to do?"

"Wait for the future, dear brother!"

"SHIT!"

❧

It was already too late. Their mother, who looked tense, became surprised when she saw that they both were playing *kawwa udd*! (A traditional game in which fingers are raised when a bird's name is recited quickly).

"Do you even know what is going on?"

"Don't disturb!" Vikram replied coolly. "We are coming for dinner."

She left without another word.

"Let's go," Vijay said while sighing, "I am really hungry!"

"Of what?" he asked, with one eyebrow raised up like an old odd lady.

"What?" he said and gulped.

"Nothing!" replied Vikram, smiled, and prepared to leave.

They went downstairs for dinner. Vijay felt uneasy after what Vikram said. It was dal and rice.

"What!"

"Eat whatever you have; there should not always be a choice for everything, brother!" said Vikram confidently.

Others just heard, and Vijay just ate silently. Soon after, they heard voices again! Cries! Shouts! Even firing!

It seemed that now there was the end. All were scared. Their mother told them not to go out ever.

"EVER!" Protested Vikram.

"Until this thing stops,"

"That we already know!"

Two days passed, and still no one seemed to think about the end. It was like a nightmare. Vikram was thinking, why will people fight for no reason.

Vijay and Vikram slept in one room. They had a twin bed. They often talked to each other. That night the same thing happened.

"When will it end?" asked Vijay hopefully.

"Never!"

"What do you even mean?"

"Never until someone stops it,"

"But who!"

"ME!"

"Do you know how much I miss my school?"

"I know!"

"You know what?"

"Missing the school!" he quickly said. "I also miss it. The friends and teachers and…"

"And what?" asked Vikram as quickly as he could, just blinking his eyes.

"And," he gulped, "Sports classes, of course!'"

They slept well, but others were really scared. It seemed like a serious situation. These things happened a long time ago. But no one expected this to return. It was a movement of movements. People killed each other. There was so much uneasiness all around.

Majority of people were from the two parties: Hail Hindu and Muslim Rise Party. They were the biggest enemies of each other, Kiran Mehta Singh and Abdul Majid. They were thirsty for each other's blood. People thought they were fighting for religion, but the real reason was something else.

There were curfews. Even the government wanted to control the situation, but things were getting worse and worse. People were losing control. Babies were killed. Women were killed. Men were… Actually, men killed them all.

The two religions could have lived peacefully, and even many people love each other. But due to some people, the two religions are meant to hate each other. We have to live in fraternity. Why war and hate?

We hate them, and they hate us, but do we ever try to see around?

When we talk well or they talk well, we never hear that sound;

They say they are good, and we say we are good every time here,

But can't we see how others suffer because of us around here and there;

We take swords, spades, rifles, and guns to take him,

Even if he isn't the one, because the light we have is dim;

Saving our souls, we take down others with wrong intentions,

But if we had tried to die for some good inventions;

Life is one and others don't have much to do what they want,

We just act like we are a stupid freaking bot;

Can we end this era and start a new one with love?

Or should we wait for some time rather than now;

We don't want others to get hurt, nor do they want us to get.

Not all, but some, are the disease here, and I bet;

We are one, and we are one, and we are one, all the time, everywhere,

But why don't we just fend each other with love and care;

If we stand together, we can rule the whole world together again.

We can just live and eat with each other, ending all the pain.

The people were freaked out because the killings were not stopping. There were hundreds of deaths everywhere. It seemed not to end. Vikram was now really wanting to end it himself, but what he could do was watch everything silently, and that is the biggest problem of this society.

"What a society!" said Vikram to Vijay when he told him the same.

"This is just from eras!"

"Bitch society!" replied Vikram with frustration. "Everyone just talks or keeps silent. Why won't someone dare to really act on this?"

"Listen I…"

"What we listen to is from eras! No, this is the reality and reality is always bitter!"

"What is the reality?"

"That we are scared!"

❧

The riots went on for weeks. Not only did they affect society and poverty, but they also affected education.

The parents did not worry about education either, but the main concern was safety. For Vikram, his mother did not let him go out. She always watched over her both sons.

After weeks, the things did not seem to resolve. Everyone was scared but bored as well. The most was Vikram.

"Mom, why can't this just end?" said Vikram in a gloomy tone.

"*Beta* this should have ended a long time ago, but the people are not understanding!"

"Which people?"

"Some people, who don't know that their competition is not with the people of their own country, rather they should compete with other countries to make this country better,"

"True yet bitter,"

"Pitiful people are suffering outside even if they don't have any part in it."

"That means those who want things to go bad should be killed."

His mother paused for a moment and then moved her hand swiftly through his hair.

"No! No one should be punished; rather, they should be counselled to get better and not create a nuisance!"

"It is impossible in a country like India!"

"No! It is impossible only because of the thoughts of people. India is the best country you can find."

"I live here, I don't need to find!" he grinned and made his mother also smile.

"Dear ,Vikram?" she asked in a very soft tone.

"Yes?"

"Promise me one thing," she said. "I know you are very young to understand this, but still promise me."

"What?"

"Promise me that you will never take a weapon in your hands and harm a single person. Promise that you will bring a revolution but with peace and *ahinsa*."

Vikram took a pause. He thought and hesitated, but then finally said it.

"I promise!"

His mother believed that her son must bring about a revolution without resorting to weapons. She believed that these nonsensical activities would cease only if a great individual shed light on society. The majority of people are literate but not educated.

"What is the difference between these two?" asked curious Vikram.

"Literate is one who studies and gets a degree from any institute, but educated can be illiterate. An educated one is someone who knows philosophy by heart. He knows the difference between logical and illogical. He knows what is right for the people. They know actually who are not among people. They don't promote something that does harm to society. They are sometimes underestimated. In India, the importance is given to the literate, not the educated."

"But why?"

"The thinking of the people!"

"But why don't they understand?"

"Leave these things and move now."

These were the worst riots that anyone had ever seen. The most calm looked the old man.

"Dada?"

"HMM!"

"Why are people doing this?"

"For freedom and ruling as before,"

"But aren't we already free?"

"You think so!" he replied nonchalantly. "People want actual rules!"

"What actual rule? We are already good, and we have the best government."

"The thing is not about the government, son! It is about who actually rules."

"So who shall rule?"

"We!"

"How?"

"Listen, whatever is going on outside, it is fair, and don't talk about it!"

"FAIR!"

"Yes!"

"HOW?"

"They arc killing the Muslims!"

"So what will that do?"

"They will die, and we will rule."

"But they aren't ruling, and we are killing them thinking that they are ruling!"

"Listen, KID! You don't interfere, okay!"

"But other people are also dying, like Hindus, Sikhs, and even Christians!"

"Let them die, and in the end, we will rule."

"I heard that the war is between Muslims and Hindus?"

"Yes!"

"So how come we rule, we are Sikhs, right?"

"Yes, but in the end, we are all the same."

"That is what I am saying; we are all the same, whether Muslims, Hindus, or Sikhs!"

His grandfather was shocked with the answer he got. He forced him to go away to his room. But the old man was trapped in his own thoughts. He was confused about whether the kid was right, but then he ignored it. Why would he follow the thought of a little boy? He had not followed the most powerful people in his age.

The killings were becoming severe. In the news, they heard that thousands were dead. Around five thousand bodies of Muslims and some four thousand dead bodies of Hindus were found. But no one cared; all they cared about was their victory. Why can't they understand that if either of the two groups wins, it will not be a victory but rather the biggest defeat ever, thought young Vikram.

Meanwhile, his elder brother had taught him to play chess. At first, Vikram was unable to play well, but later he would play better.

The employees were tenser than ever. What about their salaries? What about their families? Most of the families had to stay hungry all days because the stores were closed. At nights, goods were sent to different families secretly. Sometimes they had to depend on one day's food for several days. Some people were found dead in their homes. When it was investigated, they found out that they had committed suicide. Due to the lack of money, food, and due to the inability to fend for the families, many young people had to take this difficult step.

Fortunately, food was coming from other states and delivered secretly. Some delivery boys, who were volunteers, were killed, but they didn't stop. People were satisfied with what they had. They had learned a very important lesson of life: Be happy with what you have and never ask for more out of greed.

Shouts and rallies were common. The shouts were frightening enough. Vikram was really scared of these things. Vijay first time saw Vikram being scared of something. The cries, the shouts, and painful scratches were piercing through Vikram's heart. He couldn't bear it, and his heart started beating as fast as it could. He had many nightmares at night and woke up in the middle of the night, then his mother made him sleep again.

Vikram shouted in the middle of the night. Vijay woke up and turned on the lights. Suddenly, the door opened, and Vikram was out of his wits.

"Oh, dear! What happened?" asked his mom in a tense way.

"Vikram shouted very loudly, but I don't know why," replied Vijay.

"Those firing sounds. Men in my room are killing…"

"Ok," said his mom quickly when she understood what the problem was.

"Come on, dear. I will make you sleep again,"

She somehow made him sleep, but this happened not just once, but many times!

❧

Vikram always thought, what need of the government is if they can't stop this. prime minister was too efficient, but it was out of control. He always tried to help and stop this thing, but the power of people is more than enough. Some people even tried to kill police forces which were set out to help the needy. It was not less than a nightmare for the whole country. Debates were common everywhere.

"These people can only talk," said Vijay, "they can't act upon it!"

And he was right. People just said that it must be stopped but never said how. Some even were in favour of it. Some Muslim leaders were against the views of Hindus and some Hindu leaders were contrasting the views of Muslims.

"Is it ever going to stop?"

"No!"

6

The Great Indian Massacre

It was recorded as the most dangerous and deadly riot in the history of the world. Innocent people, when they couldn't find any other way, joined the war and ended up being killed. It was going on and no one could figure out the solution. Everything that mattered now for others was safety. The safety of their children. No one wanted to go outside. There were many occasions at that time in which the participants of the riots raided some houses. They didn't care if they were their own people. But the problem was that the family of Vikram had not imagined that the same would happen to them!

It was a pitch-dark night. Surely the cries and shouts were there, but now people were getting used to them. It was Vikram who was prepared for the raid. He imagined these things.

The lights were out for several weeks, and people had to rely on kerosene lamps, which also went out when the kerosene ran out.

That night was cold. Everyone was sleeping except Vikram as he was thinking about something. Suddenly, he heard a bang. He was alert and scared as well.

He jerked his mother's shoulders and woke her up. He used to sleep with his mother for some time because of his nightmares.

"What is it now?" she said with a sleepy voice.

"There is someone inside!"

"Come on, sleep now,"

"Why would I be joking?"

She sighed and suddenly gave a huge squeak. It was a man, a fully-grown man. He seemed to be around middle age. His face was covered. He had a large katana with him. He looked confident and angry. And to Vikram's surprise, he knew him. He had seen him somewhere. Then he talked with a hoarse voice, and Vikram was sure who he was.

"Rathore Singh's house, huh?"

It was none other than Abdul Majid! He was the leader from the Muslim side. Then, he took his mask off. Vikram's mother was out of her wits. Her blood pressure was abnormal at that time; she could feel it, but what mattered was safety.

"Why are you here?" said Vikram accidentally, and he choked after a second.

"Great confidence!" said Abdul Majid with an unusual grin and evil smile.

Vikram was silent as his heart was in his throat. Suddenly, the old man and the two brothers came. It was Vikram's father who spoke first.

"Majid!" he said with anger.

"Yes, Rathore!" he replied and touched his deadly sword with his hand.

Vikram could feel the coldness of the environment. It was spooky. He was held tight by his mother. Vikram had thought about the death of his family now. The fierce look of Majid! Vikram was feeling trembled, but suddenly his inner voice called. Why are you feeling scared? Who the hell is this Majid? You are fearless and you can defeat him easily! But he stopped thinking and continued watching the scene. He could feel sweat on his legs.

"Why are you here?" said Vikram's father fearlessly. Vikram could feel his father's energy in him.

"WHO THE HELL ARE YOU TO PROVIDE MUSLIMS WITH FOOD THAT IS…"

"What? It is not your work!"

"Nor is it yours," he replied coldly. Within no time, Vijay also reached the spot, shocked.

"I am helping them, and who the HELL ARE YOU TO TELL ME ABOUT MY WORK!"

"You are nothing but a bitch of a bastard!"

It was enough to boil the blood of Vikram. He knew he was little, but he also knew that he wasn't. He could feel the temperature rising and his eyes going red. He stood up, forcing himself out.

"I will burn you in no time, Rathore!"

He took out his sword and started to move towards Rathore Singh with determination. He was almost going to hit him when something unexpected happened. Vikram jumped on him and with all his might pressed Abdul Majid's eyes. He cried and then threw Vikram back. He didn't stop and ran towards him, hitting his pelvis.

He was knocked down and cried out in pain. Vikram could feel something sharp on his arm. It was bleeding. He had been hit with the sword.

They all ran outside. They moved without any resources. They were in haste and decided to just run. At the same time, many people were rushing towards them. They thought that they wanted to kill them, so they ran with all their might.

They were panting but didn't stop. It was the whole family: Vikram, Vijay, their parents, their uncle, his three children, his wife, and the old man.

"WHERE IS MOTHER?" shouted Rathore Singh loudly.

"She was…" the old man stopped running.

"WHERE IS SHE?"

"She is still sleeping!"

They knew that they had already lost one member. It was the worst night. Rathore and Mohan were broken. After all, she was their mother. Mohan was living alone with them. His wife and children were in their maternal home.

They still walked. They couldn't bear to move any more. They thought they were going to be killed. Suddenly, all the men and women approached them.

"What are you doing?" said one of the men.

"What?"

"They have broken into houses, run towards the temple!"

They knew that they didn't want to kill them. They were also common people. Without any more ado, they also moved towards the temple. The people were running for their lives. They wanted to be safe in their own country.

The temple was very large. It could hold thousands of people. It was safe, as Muslims wouldn't like to come there. They were moving very hard. After a long run, they all reached the temple. It was calm there.

They all settled somewhere. The Singh family was in the centre of a group. They were amazed to see that not only Hindus or Sikhs were in the temple, but Muslims were also there. One family was near them.

"Why did you come here? They won't kill you, right?" said Mohan Singh.

"You don't know them, sir!" a man replied. "They will kill anyone for their satisfaction."

"But why?" said Mohan again.

"They want their rule, and another party wants their rule!"

"This is all nonsense!" said the old man while Rathore was sitting in a corner, sad. They knew that he missed his mother, but it was fate.

It was safe there, they thought. Others also felt the same because some Muslims were also there.

"Why did you jump, Vikram?" suddenly his mother reminded everyone.

"What do you think?" he said confidently. He was bearing pain and didn't want to show anyone. He believed that it was a sign of man.

"I could have been killed." said Vikram's father quickly.

"You saw he objected to helping Muslims!" she continued, "How can he do so when he says that he wants to help Muslims?"

"It is just nonsense! This is illogical. We have the government right?" replied new member Vijay.

"I feel something is wrong." said Vikram uneasily and then told his mother to scratch his back as usual.

"I think we should sleep now," said the old man. Everyone agreed and slept on the hard surface.

The only one who couldn't sleep again was Vikram. He thought about something again. He now felt the same coldness there. The surroundings were not as usual. They seemed scary and unacceptable. He then got straight on his back and sat there with the support of the wall behind him. He could see thousands of people. They were different. Some were black, brown, and white. Some were Singhs, Khans, and Sharmas. Some were Hindus, Muslims, and Sikhs. Some were Brahmans, so-called Dalits, and others. But he could see that they all were still the same. Together when in danger. Together when happy. Sleeping openly together. No objection with each other. They were humans. They belonged to one caste, creed, and generation.

Vikram believed in the faiths of Muslims, Hindus, Sikhs, and Christians. He was unusually different. Nature had planned something else for him. He could feel his heart beating fast.

He could see that no bird was making noise. The only noise was in his head. He was thinking about the future of India. He believed that if by fate he remained alive, he would turn India around. He would bring a revolution. He would show his family that he was worth it.

Suddenly, his mother pushed him down and told him to sleep. He slept and he couldn't notice when he felt sleepy and eventually slept.

The next day, they all woke up. It was a cloudy morning. It seemed that it would rain anytime soon. But they were ready to face the rain. They just wanted peace. They did not have any breakfast. They were still satisfied with that.

Discussions started again. There was still a ray of hope. There was still the Almighty to protect. Whatever is done is for the betterment of the future.

"How?" asked Vikram to her mother when she told him the same.

"Because He is the best planner," she said softly.

They were all together, and it seemed to be the best moment of Vikram's life.

❧

When it is beautiful to remain just to remain.

When it is best to be together in harsh rain,

The beauty itself lies in the beauty of others.

When we are together through all the hot summers,

No one asks why and how; it is just as it is.

*The beauty is the creation, and it is **His**,*

Come with me, and I will show you how bees are.

We are still killing each other just for a car,

It is hard to be like the one who is odd.

You will say so, and surely everyone will nod,

Why are we dividing each other just for fun?

Why aren't we using a pen, but a gun?

It seems like a joke to most of us here.

But think about it and feel, it is rare!

Vikram was gloomy. He was missing his past. He had always believed that the past is meant to be forgotten, but now he understood that no, it is not.

It was already 12 o'clock. They were all hungry. There were not enough supplies to feed everyone. It felt like a big test by God.

The world was just changed in a moment for all of them. They still could hear gunshots and cries. The police were beaten, how could they beat them? They had illegal guns, swords, and many harmful weapons. Vikram could feel something in his pocket. There were two things: a mini knife and a pen. He was relieved to see something good. He took the mini knife and carved the date on the wall. Then he wrote. It took him half an hour, and he couldn't even feel it.

'I am Vikram Rathore, the son of Rathore Singh. I am here on a very bad day. People are killing each other. We have taken refuge in this temple. They all are outside doing whatever they want. We are here, thousands. All religions. We are together in a moment of chaos. We are one and others won't understand it. Why are the killings happening? One radical raided our house last night. I managed to defeat him. Then we all ran to this temple. I don't know for how much time we are here but it feels safe here. If anyone reads this, thank God that you are still alive. Life is not given to everyone. Live it, don't just spend it.'

He was amazed at his own wording. He was not able to understand how he managed to write it. At that time, he understood the meaning of life. Many thoughts came to his mind. He was struggling to stop thinking. He thought about how he felt so free when there was no tension about anything. While he was writing, he was thinking about nothing. He realised how happy a person can be if and only if they are satisfied with little things. No one can ever bribe a person who is happy with a small house, food, and simple clothes. He, at that time, knew what he was thinking. He was really relaxed after he wrote on the wall. It had no colour, he thought. He still was unsure about their safety.

"Are you hungry?" asked his mom and moved her hand over his head gently. He felt more positive.

"No," he replied calmly, "Not yet."

"Okay," she replied with an unusual tone, "When you feel, do tell me."

He agreed and smiled internally. Surely, they were not jovial at that time, but still they were all happy about their present. The only one who knew that danger had not vanished was Vikram.

He was feeling very thirsty.

"Mom?" he said while patting her back.

"Yes!" she replied again, calmly.

"I am feeling thirsty," he said with an odd face. Vijay was there, and he felt very weak.

"Go and drink from the washroom," she replied and continued to talk with the women with whom she already was talking.

He knew that it was not the purest water he could find, but it was also not a moment to question. Thinking of more philosophy and motivating himself, he went towards the bathroom. He went inside and closed the door. He wanted to get fresh and decided to pee there. He opened the tap. To his surprise, there was no water. He was gloomy. He couldn't bear the thirst.

He was peeing when something even more terrible happened.

There was a rush outside. He decided to peek through a hole. He was finished. He was numb. He couldn't feel his legs. There were hundreds of people with swords!

They were killing each other. Blood was everywhere. It was the worst thing Vikram had ever seen. His heart was beating the fastest ever. He knew his end had come. He wanted to accept it but he couldn't. He saw the blood and he saw the struggle; he was dawned. When he peeked again, more people came. But the problem was that they had guns. When the first gunshot was fired, Vikram fainted. He could just hear some shots for a while when he was completely unconscious.

He opened his eyes. He felt a sharp pain in his head. He seemed to move here and there. He thought of nothing but his family. Without thinking anything, he opened the door and jerked outside. He was full of tears. Tears were falling endlessly on his cheeks, and he shouted.

There was blood everywhere. Thousands of people dead in front of his eyes. He could see the river of blood flowing. Those who killed them were also dead. Guns were everywhere. He took a gun, it was a pistol. It was very heavy. He put it on his head. He thought for some time. He thought about the best moments of his life. He thought about his best satisfactions. He shot the fire. At the right time, he moved the gun in the air and it jerked his hand backward with such a great force. He realised that he was not scared of the bullet but he was scared of his death. *He felt that he couldn't kill himself.*

He moved onwards. Then it dawned on him. He saw his family. The old man, his stomach was full of blood and some body parts were out. He was crying. He saw his uncle and some related cousins. They were dead. One of his cousin's head was blown up. His hands were trembling incredibly. He could feel it. He saw his father, his father lay dead. It was his most heart-breaking incidence. He knelt and put his head on his father's body. He cried. He kissed his dad. He remembered his father's smile. His greatest moments with him. It made him, no word for that. He wanted to die but was scared. He saw his mother. Her eyes closed. Blood everywhere. He slept near her. He talked to her.

"Hey, mom," he said with hiccups and tears. "I am thirsty, give me water."

"Reply, I am hungry. Give me food. You said…"

He cried again. He remembered his brother. He stood up, but he was nowhere to be found. He couldn't find him.

"Where are you?" he cried and knelt down again near his father.

He could feel the terror. He could feel the coldness. He could feel the pain. He could feel the anger. He knew that until he does not kill, he won't rest. He knew whom to consult. He saw again in his mother's eyes. Had he ever thought about this? He was broken. He couldn't feel his eyes. Where will he go? What will he do?

He dragged their bodies. He ran to the temple. He reached a room where there were all such tools. He searched every corner of it. He heard some *thud* in a cabinet, but he didn't mind and continued to search for a shovel. He found a shovel. He had seen many people do this.

He took it and went outside. Then he suddenly saw the note he had written. He had thought that it had no colour but now, now it had a colour. It had blood. *A note of blood.*

He dragged the old man. Everyone. One after one. He managed to pile them up. He sat near them. He was crying. He felt his heart was feeling hard. It seemed to be made of stone. He dug the ground. He could not feel tiredness. He made several graves. He threw them in one by one. He covered everyone except his mother and father. He kissed them. Hugged them. He cried and talked with them. He was mentally disturbed at that time.

He somehow managed to bury them. He put soil on them. It is not easy to do so. He felt he was going to die anytime, but his fear of death stopped him. He sat there for the whole night. He was singing. He was singing a traditional song. He had lost everything. He was alone. He couldn't even find his brother's body. He went on the top of the temple and saw. He saw dead bodies. Dead families. Blood. He saw terror. He actually felt it. Not there but inside him. He knew that he had to take revenge. Tears couldn't come up. He forgot everything and then came down. He checked everybody. He took out money and all the essential things he needed. He stood up. He was still not a teenager. But he felt mighty. He didn't know how he couldn't feel sad or happy or anything else other than angry. He felt that anger was the most powerful weapon and emotion of all time.

He sat down. All his thirst had vanished. He knew that finally the riots were over for people, but for him, it had just started.

He cried. He shouted. He couldn't feel pain in his arm now. It was still bloody. He wanted serious things. He saw a man. He had a sword. He didn't want to know his religion. He was breathing!

"Sa-ve me!" he said, trembling and hardly breathing.

"You have killed many people, right?" Vikram replied coldly.

"Sav…"

Without any further ado, he picked up a gun. It was loaded. He pulled the trigger and hit the man in the head. He fell down with the gun due to its recoil. He felt uneasy after he heard that loud sound. The man had killed many people before. He felt satisfied. He could see the shattered pieces of the muscles of that man, full of blood and a big hole in his head.

He was becoming something unexpected. A middle-aged boy studying in fifth grade. He killed a man. He wanted revenge. He wanted more deaths. He wanted more terror. He was turning into a beast. Where will destiny lead him? What will he become? What will he do? What will he take revenge for? Whom will he kill? Whom will he save?

He took the gun again. He fired into the air and laughed madly. It was for sure that he was a psycho. A little fifth grader and a psycho. Unbelievable. Is the future in danger? His intentions were not good. He wanted something. He wanted revolution. But he wanted it madly. He wanted it with bloodshed and all the maddest possible ways. He finally looked at the graves he had just made himself. He smiled and left the temple.

Was this the moment that he broke the promise he had made.

PART 3

7

The New Era

"A dreadful incident had just taken place. There were only dead bodies and some suspicious graves!" said a reporter, pointing to another one.

"Yes, for sure! The riots have ended but with a great loss. The worst massacre ever recorded in India!"

He replied gloomily.

"It will be noted in the history of histories!" he replied. People were watching it on television in the teashop. They felt bad. There was also a boy watching. He was smiling and washing the utensils.

"Hey!" shouted the shopkeeper, who was around 40. "You have taken tea worth 20 rupees. Work harder."

He smiled and started banging the utensils. The shopkeeper thought he was a mad boy and was homeless.

"Do one thing!" said the shopkeeper again. "Leave!"

The boy again smiled and left without saying a word. The shopkeeper ignored him. He was sure that he was literally mental and was worth nothing.

The boy was alone. He seemed like an ordinary Indian beggar boy. No one cared much about them. The were was normal after all. But there was something special about the boy, and that was he didn't beg. He worked. He was young. He roamed everywhere. He didn't have a permanent residence.

He spent much time like this. He didn't mind being poor. He was happy. He was wandering just like a lost bird with no feathers.

But after all, he had his own identity. He wasn't identity-less. He was Vikram Rathore, a boy with no past known to anyone. He was not using his name much. He couldn't feel sadness. He was truly alone.

He was roaming in the street when he saw some dogs moving around a dead dog.

'These people don't care about anything,' he thought to himself, 'I am curious about the future of our country.'

He went there and moved the dogs away fearlessly. He dragged the dead dog with the help of polythene. The dogs stared at him. He knew that dogs understood him but humans didn't. Humans should have learned from dogs. A human has lost all his dignity, thought Vikram.

Then he moved ahead and, to his great surprise, he saw that some people were taking a dead body near Ganga.

"Rest in peace," said a man with a sad appearance.

Vikram smiled and replied with no hesitation or fear.

"Why rest in peace? Why not *live* in peace?" he said with a bright face.

"Move, kid," he said angrily, "don't know from where these beggars come from!"

Vikram smiled and moved on. He didn't mind people abusing him. He knew that it wouldn't do him anything. He was realising day by day that the social conventions are illogical. He knew that people don't do it on purpose, they do it for satisfaction. They do it to show off. But he was sad also. Not because he was poor or he was alone. He was sad because he knew he was not getting any education. He had collected some money and bought a book. He completed it. But then he couldn't save money for books because he had to eat and buy some clothes. He didn't beg. He even collected garbage for two reasons. One was food and the other was cleanliness. A young boy, beloved to his family, was not known to anyone now.

He had a small bag. He had all his things in it. He had some shirts and one pair of trousers inside it. He had a notebook and a pen. He wrote whatever he learned. He didn't go to school. How could he? He was in total misery, but he didn't mind.

He went to a shop. He wanted to do some work. He wanted some money for food and a new notebook. Fortunately, he didn't have to get money because it was a stationery shop.

"Hello, sir!" he said with a very positive attitude.

"Hello, kid!" replied the man sweetly. "What do you want?"

"Sir, I want some work, and in return, I want a notebook and a pen."

"Why?" he replied confusedly. "What work? You need a notebook, buy it!"

"Sir, I would have a long time ago, but I don't have any money,"

"Do you have any relatives or a home, you know?" he asked with an odd face.

"Yes, sir, I have a home and many relatives!" he replied confidently.

"Where and who?" replied the man in the same tone.

"My home is India, and my relatives are all good people on earth."

The man looked amazed. He was shocked as well. A boy of such a tender age, such innocence. He knew he was homeless, but his answer inspired him.

"Listen, I will give you notebooks and whatever you need, but you don't need to work," he said sweetly. He could have refused because he could trick him. But all he wanted was a notebook.

"Sorry, sir!" he replied sadly. "I won't take it if you don't let me work."

The man again looked at the appearance of the boy. A thin boy with old, torn-out clothes and a rubber slipper. Untidy hair and visible veins.

"Do you study anywhere?" asked the man without noticing that he had changed the topic.

"No," replied Vikram gloomily.

"I know you don't have money, but you can study at a government school; it is free," said the man with confidence.

"If I study, then from where will I get money for survival?" replied the boy softly.

This answer broke the man. He was disheartened. He realised life. He realised many things just because of a young boy.

"Promise me you won't refuse my deal!" said the man finally, with all the courage.

"But…"

The man stopped him and reminded him again about what he had said.

"OK! Tell me," said the boy when he had no other choice.

"You will study wherever you want, and I will provide you with money!" said the man. He knew he wouldn't change the world with this, but he could change the world for the young boy.

"OK," replied the boy without any hesitation.

He went to a school. The man took him to his own home. He treated him like his own son. The boy studied very hard. He learned all the things. After all, he had gotten a family.

The family was not very big. It consisted of the man, his wife, who without any hesitation accepted the boy, and his two sons. They played and learned together. He thought that finally he had found happiness in his life. He believed that now he was happy.

He ate delicious food. He was very intelligent. He was very smart. His body began to recover. He was becoming healthy. His life changed. If he had chosen the way of stealing and begging, he would have remained the same, but his one wish changed his life; it was education.

He read all the novels he loved. He was satisfied because he knew how to get satisfied with little things a long time ago. However, there still was a problem. He used to get nightmares. Almost once a week, he got the same nightmare. He saw a dream, a horrible but true one. He saw the massacre. He saw his family dead. He saw the graves and blood, and then he woke up and sweated a lot. His new family was really confused about that.

"What do you see in the dream?" asked the man once.

"I see myself jumping from a temple," he bluffed. He knew that telling the truth would not benefit.

He was still happy. He seldom thought about the past. He won many competitions in school. He didn't go to any government school but a private one. The school where the other two boys went. Vikram used to call the man, *papa*.

"But is not India a socialist country?" asked Vikram curiously. The man liked him because he was inquisitive.

"Yes, but now the trend has changed," he replied to him.

"But is it against the constitution, right?" he asked once more. The man was getting happier.

"Listen dear, this is India, no one believes anything!" he replied and made the boy disappointed.

❧

He was twelve years old. He was the happiest among the richest with all the riches because of all the fate had to give him. The new family was now his family. He learned many things. He was the topper. He was in 8ᵗʰ grade. The family appreciated him very much.

The two sons of the man also appreciated him. One was studying in 11th grade. He was tall and slim. He had a beard. The other was in 9th grade. He was also slim but not very tall.

They were together and loved each other. He felt a sense of belonging there. He travelled with them. He ate in restaurants with them. But he did not trouble them because he knew that he was still a stranger to them and their hearts wouldn't truly accept him.

It was a cool night. They were in the living room and watching TV.

"Can I ask you something?" dared Vikram to ask, which he hadn't dared to do until now.

"Yes?" the man replied normally.

"You didn't tell me anything about your parents," said Vikram, almost ready to be thrown out. He had recovered from that numbness by living in a family with love.

"My mother is dead, and my father is in jail," he replied quickly.

"OH!" he remarked and didn't dare to ask more. 'Why would his father be in jail?' he thought. Then he answered himself and thought he might have done some crime. There is no trust in anyone nowadays. Life is hard. So many nuisances. They watched the movie and enjoyed it. They ate popcorn. They talked with each other. They joked and there was nothing more Vikram would ask for. He was happy. He had everything. He had books, he had education and after all a loving family.

He believed that he would be an iconoclast for society. He would reform society. That was his aim. His aim was not to be a doctor or engineer but a reformer. He believed that India could touch glory in the skies. All it needed was a legend, and it was him!

⟨❦⟩

He went to school in the early morning. He didn't even mind living in a Muslim family. He had learned many prayers from there. He even knew how to read the Koran. He liked being taught anything. The main problem for him was the diet. They sometimes, if not frequently, bought meat. They bought chicken and all that but he did not eat it. He did not like eating animals. They didn't even mind. They were always ready to prepare anything for him and that is what he admired the most.

It was Monday. They were preparing to leave for school. For a reason, they hated Monday like everyone. (Vikram once said, "It is Monday tomorrow, this thought ruins my Sunday!" and made everyone laugh.)

That time he had to bring some form to school. He quickly brought it to his father.

"*Papa!*" he gasped. He was breathing heavily. He carried a notebook in his hand.

"What is the matter?" he replied, "You look haggard!"

"I—" he breathed heavily and continued, "want you to fill out the form," he said and calmed himself down.

The man took the form and read it. His face turned upside down. He looked pale.

"What is the matter?" said Vikram with a furrowed brow.

"Hmmm!" he replied to hide his real intention. He took the form and wrote something on it. Vikram was also happy, but the problem was that he did not know what he wrote on the paper. He thought he was filling the form. He took the form quickly, wrapped it in his bag without checking, and left. They all caught the bus on time. They talked and enjoyed the ride. All his classmates on the bus showed him their forms. But his bag was on top of a grill in which bags are kept. He didn't want to waste his energy on bringing down the bag and then putting it back.

They reached the school. They walked together to the classroom. He was with his friend. He liked being with him for two reasons: one was that he was simple and charming, and the second was that his name was Varun Sharma.

They knocked on the door. There was already a teacher sitting. He was their H.R.T., he allowed them both. They went inside and high-fived with their friends and took their seats. They had P.E. that day. Some boring classes passed and then came the dreaded social science class. It was taught by a lady teacher. Her name was Priya. She came in. She was going to take their forms. She called all one by one.

"Mmm!" she remarked and then continued, "Tushar Vikalp."

A thin, tall boy stood up, handing in his form. He gave it to the teacher and then left without receiving any response. He was odd.

She called others the same way. Some were usual, and some were unusual.

"Mister!" she said, stopped and smiled. "Yes! So, Mister Vikram Rathore!"

"Yes, ma'am," he said and ran towards her. She smiled and looked towards him. She looked odd at that time.

"Your form filling is a little bit casual!" she said, smiling again. Vikram knew there was some problem. The man filled it badly.

"Listen, class!" she continued. "Listen to what is written here. Please don't give such kinds of forms. What is the need for the names of grandparents? You must look after it. Don't give rubbish forms to fill!"

The whole class laughed. Vikram went pink. It might not look very insulting, but the greatest question at that time was why had he written so?

He was not sad but was curious. He later decided not to ask the man about it. Then it was the turn of his favourite class, sports.

They went down. He was advanced in football now. He was in eighth grade, of course. They took the ball and made teams. He was in a strong team. He felt bad for the other team but he had no other choice.

Just after the kick-off, the ball was in the possession of Vikram. He took the ball without any extra effort near the goalpost. He kicked very hard, but the ball went straight out. The team was disappointed. But the other team was cheering. He didn't mind. He had missed several goals in that match, and they lost it by 2-0. They all cursed him, but they didn't know that he did it with intention. He wanted them to win.

They all left the class upon departure and reached their respective buses. He stopped thinking about the form, and they started talking about politics.

"This is absurd!" said a boy who was in eleventh grade. He patted his forehead hard.

"What is absurd?" asked Vikram and then sat comfortably.

"You see these ministers just talk on elections," he said and then pointed towards Vikram to reply.

"Yes, and that is why it is called politics!" he replied coolly, and the others laughed. The eleventh grader also smiled and turned aside. He knew that Vikram knew well about politics. They all often talked about it.

They reached home and remained as normal as they were. Vikram was reminded of telling the man about the incident, but he found it too odd, so he didn't ask. The man, on the other hand, looked amazed because Vikram didn't tell him anything about

He thought about it and then didn't worry.

Life was going smoothly. Vikram was in 8th grade (Repeated it many times, but it is just emphasising the fact that he has developed much because of love!).

He was doing well. His percentage was very good. He also spoke very well. Once a teacher told him that he could be a very good speaker. He didn't care about it. Where will speaking help him? It hardly mattered to him. His strategy making was also perfect. He knew what decision to take at which time. It also amazed the teachers. He wanted to reform the society. Will that work?

He knew that he had to think about that. He did not know how he could accomplish his goal. He was not clear about his vision.

What mattered at that tender age was brilliance. His family was supporting him. That is all he needed. But something struck in his life so bad that he had to give up everything, ranging from education to his career. He was shocked. He wanted to die again, but the fear.

He was helpless and maybe scared.

8

The Deadly Secret

He was happy until something really bad happened. It was a beautiful day. The day was Wednesday, and it was summer. The families of the whole area were normal. There was peace all around. The name of the man he was living with was Arshid Ahmad. He cared for his family well, including Vikram. Vikram wanted his support to choose a career in which there could be some reformation of society. He wanted to do it with peace.

Vikram was in school. They had a social science class. The topic was the game of nature. He was supposed to study about the worst massacre in India at that time. He was not ready to study it, but he had no choice. The teacher was erasing the board.

"Sir, I feel uneasy," he said, "can I visit the nurse?"

Surely, some boys teased him about that. They are all sensitive. They just need a topic, and they will start a parliamentary discussion on it. Meanwhile, they were teasing him and laughing from inside and smiling evilly from outside. The teacher gave a response.

"Ah!" he remarked, took a long breath and continued, "I reckon that you know that the nurse is herself ill and she has not visited the school for weeks, Mister Rathore!"

It struck him. How could he forget it? He could not make any other tantrum now because the teacher will realise what he has to realise.

"So students, now we will study about the great massacre of India!" he said, and all the students were eager to know about it except the person who himself was the part of that bloody scene. How can he forget it? Everything seemed to be fresh. He could still remember the cries and everything there. It was just as bad for him as life to the lover of death. It was not the ears listening but a soul that looks forward to collect its own shattered pieces. He might not bear the pain of the past, yet the present has to be dealt with, and he cannot escape it. It was not just a topic for him but a morass of the past which wants to sink him inside it.

Nevertheless, he has to face it and the same thing happened. The teacher started. He wrote the topic on the board, the date, the subject, and all the school conventions.

"Not long ago has this happened," said the teacher, "just a few years before."

All the students knew that well. Of course, they were born before the incident.

"It was done by some terrorist group. They came and killed everyone who was present at that time in the temple. They shot a person in the head. Some graves were there, which were later removed and corpses were thrown away. They believed that the people in the graves were part of the group. They were buried very well, and others were not. The identities were not known and are still unknown. Not even a single person managed to escape!"

All the students were shocked. They found it very amusing. They even compared it with old massacres as well. But the most confused was Vikram.

Terrorists, graves, and they are part of a group! It shocked him. The bodies of his family members were thrown away. It was unbearable. He couldn't hold it anymore.

"Sir, which organisation did research there and found the bodies?" asked Vikram with full badass energy.

"It was an NGO," he replied. "The name is People's Party of Peace, or we call it PPP. Even though it has 'party' in it, it is not the same."

He knew it now. He could not bear the name of the organisation. How can they do this? They don't even know what had happened. It is all illogical. So much disgust all around. Any fucking NGO will come and declare anything; this is just shit.

He reached home with a terrible mood. This was now going out of control. What is the fun? He just wanted to destroy the whole party. He had now decided that he would enter politics in the future. He would become the deserving minister and do whatever he wanted to do. He just wanted power now. He wanted authority. He wanted revolution. He wanted to become a paradigm. He wanted to destroy fake parties. He wanted to create his own kingdom. He wanted to rule. He wanted revenge. He wanted everything anyway, whether peacefully or by taking a gun in his hands. He could kill millions to save billions.

His mentality was changing again. He was again being something he never meant to. He was just breaking his mother's promise.

He wanted justice by doing injustice. He wanted peace by ways of war. *If you want peace, prepare for war!*

He had thought everything. He had decided what to do. He was ready to face the world. He knew that he was not ordinary. He knew that he was the legend.

They all were tense. Two days had passed and Arshid Ahmad was not home. They called everywhere. They checked everywhere. He was nowhere. It was again a big problem. Vikram knew that his life was never meant for peace. Would he ever be successful in bringing peace? The main job was now finding the lost man. He knew that there was some problem from the beginning. His wife was crying. She couldn't bear her husband being lost, of course. Vikram knew that this was going now out of hand. He was fed up with life. He hated tension. He wanted to relax but life didn't want him to be.

"We shall go to the police," recommended Vikram to the woman, Shafia, "we can file an FIR and the police will do its work."

"I think he is right," said her brother. He was present at that time. "We shall go to a police station."

There was no other choice. They had to go to the police station. They entered the police station.

"Hmm," remarked a policeman who was busy with some work. "Lost! Sit down for a while."

They did the same. The whole family was there. Vikram was tense. Everyone was. It was like a nightmare. Where could he go? Thought Vikram.

"Let the SP *sahib* come," he said and put a whole *paan* in his mouth and continued with a very fat voice, "he will look into the case."

That was another problem now. The police. He has to file a FIR and that is it. No! He has to bring the prime minister himself to fill it. That is absolutely disgusting. Vikram was feeling an urge to kick the fat man in the face, but then he controlled himself. He couldn't watch a fully-grown woman crying and the policeman finding it amusing.

"Sir, it is urgent," said his brother, who had a black beard and tall height. "What are you doing?"

"Don't try to argue," he replied ragefully, "you will not teach me my work."

The other man was silent, the least he could do. No one was coming. The fat man was chatting. Vikram was out of his wits. His anger could strike anytime into fully-grown rage. He had seen it himself just once in his life. He just did not want it to emerge again. He was heating from inside. A woman crying, children tense, and that son of a bitch enjoying on the phone.

"It is getting late!" said Vikram in a high pitch so that the fat man could hear him.

The fat man stood up. He pointed to his name on his shirt. He swallowed something and touched his hair.

"Hey, brat! Shut up!" he said with an overconfident attitude. Vikram was now out. He was ready to bust him. "Shut the FUCK up!"

That was it. He stood up. He went to the other side with full rageful emotion on his face. He went near a big board on which there were big sticks. He took one out. He walked hastily towards the man and then he did it. He hit him in the leg. The big monster cried. Then he hit his phone. The phone was broken. The others were now hopeless of even finding themselves again. Vikram hit him nonstop.

"I am what?" he said with breaks while he was hitting a person ten times bigger than him. He was truly a beast. He seemed to have no mercy. His teeth were clenched tightly, and the cries of the policeman attracted others as well.

"STOP!" said the woman's brother. But he was unaware about Vikram. He was not going to stop. The other policemen came and tried to break up the fight. Even though at one point Vikram was pulled out, he still hit with the stick. He hurt some other officers too.

"YOU ARE NOT DOING ANY FUCKING WORK AND TELLING ME WHO I AM!" he shouted as hard as he could. He didn't care if he was sent to jail. He just wanted to kill the half-dead man. The other man could not even move his leg. He seemed to be unconscious.

"STOP!" shouted the policemen, and then somehow the show stopped. They pulled him out. They all cursed him. They pulled up the fat man and made him comfortable. The fatso could not even talk. Vikram had truly shown him the power of a common man. The other policemen seemed nice, but that bastard was just unbearable.

❧

Everything was settled and all was calm except the fatso was taken to the health centre. It seemed awfully funny that a small boy just half killed a fatso large policeman with full training.

The family members were upset with him. The lady was sometimes watching him, sometimes watching her husband's photo. Sometimes, she was crying and sometimes she was silent.

They could not bear him. Finally, they were called to fill the form. They filled it and a policeman came to ask some questions to them.

"When did he leave home?" said the police officer with a serious mood.

"At morning."

"Is that his usual timing?"

"Yes."

"What does he do?"

"A shopkeeper."

"What kind of?" he said. "I mean, what does he sell?"

"He is a bookseller."

"OK! Now I want you to tell me about his whole family."

"His name is Arshid Ahmad. I am his wife, Shafia Jan. He has two children, Aslam and Atif."

"Who are they?" he asked while pointing to the man and Vikram.

"OH!" she said regretfully. "The boy is…" She couldn't continue saying it.

"Adopted," continued Vikram himself. It amazed everyone.

"That man?"

"He is my brother,"

"Arshid Ahmad? His parentage?" he asked while thinking.

"His mother has passed away; she was Amtul Jan."

"What about his father?"

She hesitated at first, but then collected all the courage to answer. This was the moment that Vikram truly wanted to die.

"His father is alive, and he is - ah! - Abdul Majid!"

It struck Vikram. He didn't want to hear any more. He had been living with his enemy for years. How come he couldn't get it before? When the teacher read the note, when the man told him while watching television, he was full of hate at that time. He wished that they would never find the man again. He hoped that he was dead because soon he would be sending a father to a son for a meeting.

He was fed up. He was full of anxiety. He was just fed up with life. He was pressing his hands so hard that they could have broken. Without wasting any more time, he decided to leave the place. He left the station without letting anybody know about his absence. He was done. He just wanted to live alone. He didn't want any more people to come into his life. He had already faced what an 80-year-old wouldn't have. He was done. He was ready to beg but not live with them again.

He could just think of what he thought before meeting the man. He wanted what he wanted a long time ago. He was not going to be silent. He wanted deaths. He wanted a massacre again. He was mad. His brain was not going just as it should have gone. Why? His life was playing games with him. God seemed to make fun of his life. For a moment, he stopped believing in God but then realised that that is not fair. But his anger still was not down. He was now going for what no one would have ever wanted to do in one's 8th grade. He wanted to kill Abdul Majid, and it was his first step. But the problem was that he did not know in which jail he was. He had to find it out. Whatever it might take, he was ready to give.

His heat was now burning his body as well. He picked up a stone from the road and threw it as hard as he could at a dog. The dog cried out loud because of pain, and it gave the little boy pleasure. What was his mistake now? He wanted to kill everyone, but first of all, he wanted to start with the old bastard. Everything was over now. He was alone, and he was free. He could do whatever he wanted to do. He had great endurance; now it was time for action.

He wanted chaos. He wanted to be the king of chaos. He knew that he was wrong and someone would definitely be there to stop him, but he didn't care. He was going to bust him as well. He wanted to collect some money first. His ambitions were not great. He walked hungrily to another city. It took him two days and now he wanted a fresh beginning.

He was pitiful about his own life. But he believed that he would soon do the destined thing. The revolution was out of his mind. He wanted something not less than what a criminal wants, a terrorist to be more specific!

9

The Way of Politics

The small boy was now 24. He was really close to the thing he wanted. He wanted to go into politics. He had just one more year to be eligible for elections. He had even created his own party, at that time led by Abdul Majid. The party's name was 'The Legend's Club'; it surely was a unique name. But the problem was recognition. The party needed to be known by everyone.

He was a candidate from the Varanasi constituency. First, he wanted to be an MLA. After that, he could go for higher positions and after a long journey, become the prime minister. But it was only possible if he consistently won the elections. Fortunately, just a year later, there were the state elections. The most important thing at that time was winning the hearts of the people of Varanasi. For that purpose, he needed money, and he already had it.

"What do you think, old man?" he said, pointing to Majid. "How much should we devote to bribing?"

"I think," he said, and gave an evil smile, "maybe around 6 crores."

"Maybe less," he said, and turned his left cheek up.

"Then how about 20 crores?" he said and started writing something on his phone.

"Ah!" he said and gave a small laugh. "You jumped really high, but yeah, that will work."

Then it was done. They had money. They had everything. Now they just wanted to create campaigns. Surely, the elections were far away, but still,

"I think, first of all, we should post banners all around," recommended the old man.

"Yes, but the quality of banners should be next level," replied Vikram and was busy with some other work.

"How much should we invest?" asked the old man with the phone in his hand.

"Look, you don't need to stick all over Varanasi," he replied. "Stick it on large billboards; I will take them from Manoj."

"Who is Manoj?" asked the old man, diverting the topic.

"Your father, Manoj!" he replied, and the old man fell silent.

They had brought large billboards. Now it was their turn to make the design, which Vikram himself took the responsibility for.

"What should we write for our slogan?" asked the old man.

"Hmm!" he replied with his left cheek up. "The slogan which we submitted, leave it there; we will use another one."

"Think about something," the old man said, even when he did not need to.

"We don't want what others want; we want a revolution," said Vikram. "Is it all right?"

"Do you really want to do something?" contradicted the old man; it was clear he didn't like it.

"We will do what no one has ever done," said Vikram and felt honoured.

"Hmm!" the old man remarked. "Cool!"

"But isn't it too normal?" asked Vikram.

"Use it!" he said firmly, and they did the same.

Abdul Majid did not use his original name. He was hidden from people. He used his name as Shekhar Banarasi. But he was the mastermind of the party. The party did not have many members. They were two and some other workers who worked for money and food only.

They installed the billboards and then their custom posters. People did not notice it too much. Now they wanted something more powerful. They needed speeches and people. They rented an auto-rickshaw and some people.

"LISTEN, EVERYONE!" shouted a man through a loudspeaker while moving through the city. "ALL OF YOU MUST GATHER AT THE BIG PLAYGROUND NEAR THE HOSPITAL. WE HAVE SOMETHING TO PROVIDE YOU!"

People were going insane. They were getting something. That was incredible. Almost all of the people decided to visit at the given time and date. They, in the rickshaw, said many other things that motivated the people even more to visit. It was actually a speech by Vikram, and he decided to provide every person with 500 rupees. In the future, they announced, if the people come and listen more, they will get more and more. It is India. How could anyone not come? Some thought there might be some trick, but only *some*.

It was the day when the speech was going to start.

They all came to the place. Some settled when a person opened the microphone and blew into it first before starting to speak.

"Thank you for coming here. This is a very important programme. At the end, you all will get 500 rupees. Those who will be consistent will be provided more and more. At the end of today's programme, there is a lottery of 10,000 rupees. And yes, only one winner. Stay tuned and stay attentive. I would like to invite on the stage the owner and the maker of the programme, Mister Vikram Rathore!"

The people cheered more than ever. They were excited for the money and the speech of the rich man. Vikram went to the dais. He also adjusted the microphone and started.

"Hello, everyone!" he said at first with a very calm mood. "I am Vikram Rathore. I will start my speech, but before that, let me tell you, I am not gonna start any formal speech. You are my people, my responsibility, and my family. You feel relaxed and yes, this is your friend, son, brother, or whatever you want to consider me, talking. I am no stranger, but I am your well-wisher. I was not in the spot till now because my age was not much. But now, I am here to address you and to tell you everything. Listen, first of all, what I am going to tell you might make you feel uncomfortable and nonchalant. I am here for elections. I am running for the MLA seat. We, The Legends Club, are a party who are not like others. If you think we are doing it for money, then no, we are already loaded. Our party is here and always here for you. We will not talk about everything a politician says. We are here to bring a revolution. We don't want your money. We want your love. I, Vikram Rathore, believe that if I get elected as the MLA of Varanasi, then you will not face any problem-"

He stopped for a while. Something else struck him. Thousands of innocent faces. Thousands of needy people. They are just like him when he needed support. He was alone and helpless. Same are they. Why will he play with them? Why will he misuse their precious votes? He will get votes but for the real things he is going to do. He decided to change. Meanwhile, people were shocked to see him stop.

"What happened? Forgot the lies?" shouted someone from the public, and there was a huge wave of sound from the public. But to his surprise, the man in front of him just smiled.

"Yes!" he replied with a happier tone. "I forgot the lines. I, being serious, wanted to give a simple speech and just bluff out things. I wanted to misuse you, the votes, but then it struck me, why? I am Vikram Rathore, someone special with something special. I have you. You are my family. I believe that a common man is the brother of another man. So, we believe in fraternity, and we will be the example that people have been talking about for centuries. I will create opportunities now. I will change the system. I will bring the revolutions. I will do whatever my people, my real people, want. I want you to speak one by one and tell me your needs."

One by one, some people stood up to speak. A young man stood up because Vikram chose him randomly. He was given the microphone.

"Hi," said the young and energetic man, "I want employment, and we are just fed up with everything. We want money for seriousness. We are fed up with the lies. We want the real revolution."

"Listen, young man," said Vikram, "you are right. I am also fed up with everything. When talking about employment, we will create. Not just talking, but let me tell you how. We can create such beautiful and innovative programmes, which won't only benefit us but the whole society. Take, for example, there are very high cases of kidnapping and they lead to many bad and horrible things.

"For that, we have an idea. Near junctions and other places, we will insert such cameras that will not only record the cars moving but will trace the car number and driver's faces as well. By chance, if something bad happens, the camera can help. And now talking about employment, we have to manage the databases and physical protection as well. Along with that, we will give young programmers a chance to showcase their skills. For that, we can have jobs. For that, we can fund people. For that, we can save many lives. We will show you people what really socialism means. We will show you how really schools and hospitals are made. We will show you how hidden, thousands of them, employment opportunities can be just traced out."

Second hand was there. It was an old man with specs.

"Dear, *beta*, we all want peace all around. There are these mafia people who are disturbing the societies. What to do?"

"Listen, uncle," he said, "we will move the police like they have never moved before. We will clear out all the gangs. We will show the gangsters the real power of the police. If they feel they are free to commit crimes, then I and we all are here to prove them wrong. We will just bust those bastards for the sake of it."

"But I think politicians hire gangsters!" someone just shouted loudly and contradicted the speaker.

"I am not a politician. People call me because that is the work. Morally, I am the revolution bringer and the saviour of my people."

There was a huge applause. People were starting to believe that someone had come to help them. He is the real help. He will surely help everyone and bring about a revolution.

"What about water, electricity?" asked someone from behind.

"We won't hide them. We won't use them for the sake. We will use them for you. But for that, I request you people to respect water. It will not come again when you need it. Why are you polluting the Ganga? Why are you wasting water? Why are you wasting electricity also? If you cooperate, then surely, everything will be provided with no selfish means."

There was again a huge applause. He seemed to be literate. He talked very well. His presence of mind seemed to be very fine. He was handsome also. His party members were also shocked. They didn't expect this.

"What about corruption?" asked someone again from behind the people.

"Corruption is not a practice. It is a habit. Believe me, those who are corrupt will be thrown away to jail, and new people, especially youth, will be requested to join the jobs. We will finish it as soon as possible. No corruption. If I get your support, your love, then there will be no such nonsense things. India will be free of these freaking things. But again, I request you not to pay extra money. If someone does so, just complain and the rest will be seen. Don't be scared of anyone; everyone is equal and equally powerful."

There was again a huge applause, and this one was large. People started getting closer to him, but he still was a fresher, so there was still a doubt on him.

"Why should we trust you?" asked someone, and this question was eagerly anticipated by many.

"That is true. Why should you trust me? Go and trust those damn losers who just talk. Believe me, you are habitual of judging people because of the prejudice of the position from the past."

This was enough. Some people just devoted themselves to him.

The people got their money, and a man even won ten grand. He was happy and had decided to vote for the man. Some, however, criticised him because they adored the other leaders, but some thought that he was going to bring a revolution. There still was time. There still was a possibility of taking the majority in.

They then went to their residence. Majid was amazed to see Vikram's speech. He didn't expect him to be like this. His acceptance of being selfish hit them hard. They were confused.

They were in the car, moving really fast.

"Why did you say that your intentions were something else?" asked Majid in an uncertain manner.

"I don't know," he replied confidently, "it just hit me and I said so."

"Amazing, but I could see a lot of hopeful faces," said Majid in a happy manner.

"I want to maintain the hope," he said. "I want to be clear and truthful."

"But…"

"You know when you broke into my house and because of that, I lost everything. I didn't even have hope, but now I am happy," said Vikram. "I know how they were feeling at that time."

"You sure about that?" asked Majid, "because then it can change everything."

"You know what I wanted from ever?" replied Vikram in a question that he answered himself. "Revolution. I can bring that. I want power. Politics is power but it might take some time."

Majid sighed and then thought to himself. Vikram, however, was happy and satisfied with his decision because he could feel it. Then they discussed advertisements and more programmes. They needed more money and luckily it was not scarce. They had hundreds of crores in general accounts, but no one knew about their hidden accounts.

❧

"What about social media?" said Vikram when they were talking about advertisements.

"Everywhere," replied Majid, who was looking at something on his phone.

Vikram was already angry. He took the phone from him and almost threw it down with great force.

"What the hell!" screamed Majid with astonishing vocals.

"I am really going to break it, focus on work and once we win the elections, then I will buy you new phones," said Vikram and smiled.

They thought that making arrangements and creating advertisements were all about elections. They didn't think about defence. The other people in elections. They did not think about what they could do. And due to their lack of attentiveness, they were almost doomed to death. It was just unexpected. Vikram could have lost his life and the old man, *almost*.

They were in a room. They were resting and looking into their phones. There were just two of them. They heard a bang outside. First, they ignored it, but Vikram decided to look outside from the window. He opened the window and WHAM!

A sword hit Vikram's arm. It was bleeding. The wound was in the same place as in the past. He jumped back and remarked on the pain.

A fully-grown man with some other men sneaked from the window with large swords. They seemed dangerous, but they did not know Vikram well.

"Hey, newcomer!" said the boss to Vikram. "Inviting people, you son of a bitch. I will tear you down in no time!"

"Really!" remarked Vikram in a cool attitude, which amazed them.

"What do you mean, man?" asked the boss, who was large but his face was hidden with a mask. His body was covered in a black costume. They were a hired gang.

"Who sent you?" asked Vikram with a warning vibe.

A man came in front of him and flexed himself.

"What do you…"

There it was. Vikram shot his leg with a gun that he had with him. Everything was clear. Everything was really *really* clear. The other men knew who the man was. Meanwhile, the shot man was squealing with pain. Vikram was smiling.

"Who sent you?" asked Vikram again with a dangerous vibe now. They were forced to speak the truth. The shot man was lying down and crying in pain. He was irksome.

"It was Sharma," said the big boss, who looked smaller than Vikram now. "It was Karan Sharma."

"From where?" asked Vikram.

"From here, Banaras."

"OK!" he pointed to the wounded man. "Who do *you* work for?"

"Karan Sharma," he replied and got another shot on the same leg. It was his big mistake that he just spoke.

"YOU ALL WORK FOR ME!" he replied. "Right?"

"Yes," replied everyone in the same rhythm and at once, while the man was now shouting out of pain, but there was no one who was going to listen to him.

"Now," he said, "I want you to do something, but I don't understand one thing."

"What?" said a man, but then immediately added, "sir?"

"People hire gangs, but they give them swords, so foolish!"

"Yes, sir,"

"Tell me one thing," asked Vikram.

"Yes, sir," said the big boss.

"Go and invite Sharma to my house for a meeting."

"But why will he come and he would kill us if he hears that we could not kil... sorry hurt you?"

"Are you a *behenchod*?" he shouted in rage and blew air towards his cut.

"NO!"

"Then go and find that bastard!" he shouted, trembling everyone.

Meanwhile, the old man was watching all this. He was aghast. He couldn't feel his legs. Vikram was bleeding, a man crying out in pain, shot twice, and in the same place. This was disgusting. He was just frightened. He wanted to call Vikram, but his voice couldn't come out of his vocal cords. This was unbelievable for him. The thought that struck him was that if he was attacked now, then how many attacks he would have to face in the future. He wanted to keep him out. He wanted to keep him out of politics. From this bullshit. He wanted to save him. He didn't want to let the world lose a legend.

"Sir!" said one man. "Of course, sir, we will find that bastard, and if he refuses to come, we will just drag him here."

"That is good, boys," replied Vikram, "Move now and bring him tomorrow at sharp 10 am."

"Of course, sir," replied the boss and left through the main door after having a cup of water. They were sent with love, but the wounded man was taken to a private hospital, and everything was under control.

❧

"Vikram, don't you think this is dangerous?" asked the old man when he was out of his trauma.

"What is dangerous?" asked Vikram in turn.

"Politics?"

"That is obviously not," replied Vikram confidently, "yeah, when we win, then there is no problem?"

"But what if we don't win?" asked the old man. "There is that Sharma, son of a bitch."

"I am going to see him now."

"He is not an ordinary guy; he has power."

"Am I ordinary?" asked Vikram, but answered himself, "Of course I am not. I am better than him."

"I know, but what when he tries to kill you again?"

"He won't dare again!"

"Ok," replied the old man, "what if someone else tries to?"

"I will kill him."

The old man closed his eyes and sighed. He knew Vikram was overconfident right now. He didn't have power, nor did he have people in support. It was truly dangerous for him. But he wouldn't listen. He did whatever he wanted to. He was just his own ruler. Yesterday he was almost dead, and today he is meeting his killer. That is total bullshit!

The doorbell rang. Vikram himself went to open the door. When he opened it, there was Karan Sharma. He looked terrible. He seemed to have been dragged for kilometres.

"Ah!" said Vikram in surprise, "Mr. Sharma from Banaras!"

"Vikram, leave me. I am sorry," cried Sharma in pain.

"I understand, but I want to talk to you, really. I swear."

"Please, I swear I won't do it again."

"Please come in. I want to talk to you about work."

He didn't believe them, so he was forced by his former workers inside the house and made to sit on a couch.

"What do you think, will you be safe after killing me?" asked Karan in a scared manner. But to his surprise, Vikram laughed very hard. He may be just pretending to laugh but it seemed more dangerous to Karan.

"Silly!" said Vikram after finally stopping the evil laugh. "I will kill you? Nonsense, why will I kill you? I want to talk about work only."

"What work?" asked Karan, still in a scared voice.

"Listen, I want to talk about the upcoming election," said Vikram in a pleasant way. Karan noticed the bandage on Vikram's arm. It looked like he had been badly wounded and he was going to take revenge. He still did not believe him.

"Elections?" said Karan and paused to think, "What do you want from me?"

"I want your party details, like where you are going for programmes and which constituencies you rule."

"Why would I tell you that?" asked Karan in an angry manner.

"Because you have to live," said Vikram coldly.

Karan gulped hard and sighed. He closed his eyes and sighed again. He knew if he didn't do it, he would be done. He had to do it. He had to tell him.

"Listen," said Karan, "our constituencies are Varanasi, Lucknow, Aligarh, Allahabad, Noida, and many more. We have around 46 constituencies. We have ruled here. We can win here."

"Hmm!" remarked Vikram and smiled a bit. "That means simply if you win your major constituencies, you become the chief minister, right?"

"Yes, maybe, yes," said Karan in a comfortable way.

"What if we form a coalition and I speak to the public? Your party, your rules, I only need your support and your background."

Karan thought a lot. He was not clear about that. He thought, why would he do a coalition with him? But then it struck him. Vikram is an efficient speaker and he has the guts to do it. If he just uses Vikram, then surely he will win and gain the power. He was satisfied and excited. His adrenaline was rushing.

"Yes," he said and smiled. "Deal done!"

Vikram smiled and shook his hand. He was happy with that. No one could help him more than himself.

"Can you give me your phone number?" asked Vikram, with his phone in his hand, out of his pocket.

"Of course, yes, take it," he said and gave him his number. Vikram saved his number as Sharma Banaras and listed him in his favourites.

"When will we announce that?" asked Karan after doing the deal.

"What?" asked Vikram, confused.

"That we are in a coalition?" asked Karan, and Vikram patted his head sorrowfully.

"Listen, man!" said Vikram, "We are not a famous party; you just hired us as your workers."

"Well, will that work?" asked Karan in confusion as he was calculating something.

"That will not just work, my dear, it will go far!" said Vikram and both smiled, "Let me do the rest and handle the affairs in my hand and see how I do the work."

"What?" asked Karan, who was again confused as well as scared when Vikram said the last words.

"Well, see, let me decide when to go for programmes and when to speak. I will also speak, but I won't be very famous in public outside our constituencies, and that will just do the magic. I will influence the people and see how they cast their votes for us."

"What about me?" asked Karan in disappointment.

"That means you will like me to become the C.M.?"

Karan smiled and understood everything. Vikram was a mastermind. He knew that if Vikram works with him, the party will rise above the clouds. If he becomes the C.M., then there is just fun.

The name of the party was Hindustan Party of Revolution, or Hindustani Inquilab Party. Their slogan was very popular, "Inquilab Zindabad" or "Hail Revolution." It was a slogan from Bhagat Singh and his companions, who were hanged by the British government. The party was already famous and now it had a new face, Vikram Rathore.

❧

"Are you MAD?" shouted Majid at Vikram for his decision.

"Listen, old man…"

"I don't want to listen to anything, young man. You make all the unnecessary decisions and leave me with nothing. You are just going mad, Vicky."

"What do you need?" asked Vikram aggressively.

"I?" said the old man. "I need power, money, and authority!"

"That is what you are getting, mad man," said Vikram.

"What do you mean?" asked the old man.

"See, we are going to represent the party, HIP, and we will get the fame. We will win the elections, and Karan will become the C.M., and we will get everything we need."

"That is fair, then," said the old man, and both laughed very hard.

❧

Vikram and the old man left their mansion. It was large and decorated very beautifully. He bought it for around 55 crores. They left for Karan Sharma. They wanted to talk further and make more decisions. They were travelling in a Ford Endeavour and were comfortable. The old man was happier. He had never thought of leaving the old dusty prison and moving in a big car. Vikram was very well-off. They finally reached Karan's house. They entered the gates and then left the car.

"Hello, Bhabhi!" said Vikram while walking through the corridor and pointed to some girl.

"*Hat Badmash!*" she said and blushed. She ran away, and Vikram smiled to himself. He was pleased.

"*Aaja sanam, madhur chandni mai hum...*" he was singing to himself until he reached Karan's room. He knocked on the door and entered the room.

The room was quite big. It had a huge library. Some books were in the history section. Some in geography. Some in political science. Some in psychology. Some in social studies and so on. Vikram really felt jealous of him. He was not even 10th pass. He was, almost. On the other hand, Karan had graduated from Oxford in business studies.

Whatever, Vikram was here to talk about politics, and he was sure that he knew politics better than he did.

"Oh! Sit down, Vikram, and you?"

"I am Ab- ah! I am Shekhar," said Majid, almost tongue-slipped, "people often call me Shekhar Banarasi."

"Well, then I know you because Vikram told me about you on the phone. I heard that you help him in his work. I bet then you are more experienced. Have you ever been in politics?"

"Leave these rubbish talks. Let's talk about our work," interrupted Vikram.

"Yes, well, if we talk about General Elections, those are far away, but state elections are just a year later. So we need to go for more agendas and attract more people."

"Leave that to me," said Vikram confidently.

"Well, about money, I don't care about that. I will provide you."

"That is done!" said Vikram, and smiled. Karan smiled back.

"Then I need a team also," added Vikram while holding a mini globe in his hand and started rotating it. He rotated it very fast and then suddenly put it back on the table with a thud.

"Yeah, I will provide you that."

"How many members?" asked Vikram and started playing with his fingers on the table.

"Around," he thought, "I don't know, what do you think?"

"Maybe 20?" he suggested as he thought telling a large number might ruin the confidence.

"That is done then," said Karan, and then they left. The old man found it odd and thought Karan is not a trustful person.

"Oh! Come on," said Vikram, "you are just a dumb old man. You saw how he just gave his money to us!"

"He has not given yet,"

"Well, he will be giving,"

"But that is not the point. See how quickly he just agreed with you," he said and started chewing his nails.

"He is scared of me; he knows one wrong move and he will be done," replied Vikram proudly.

"Listen, he is a politician; he knows more than you. He knows how to trap people."

"You think he is trapping?"

"Yes!"

"Thought about me?"

"What?"

"Did you not think how I cannot trap him?"

"What do you mean?"

They had planned a speech in Lucknow. Karan, Vikram, and the old man were in one car, whereas all the other members of the party were behind and in front of them.

"You know what to say?" asked Karan as he was worried because it was going to be his first speech.

"You think I am from the slums or whatever?"

"No, I mean, are you well prepared or not?"

"I don't need preparations!"

They reached Lucknow in no time. They had already set the stage and the tent. There was accommodation for thousands of people, and the cost of the whole programme was almost a crore.

All the people who were interested settled. Until all the seats were full, every special party member was sitting on a chair. Then the host of the meeting opened the microphone and started talking.

"Ladies and gentlemen, today we all gather here as part of the most revolutionary party, HIP. We are here to figure out today's agenda. For that, our speaker, Mr. Vikram Rathore, is invited."

There was a huge applause. No one knew him. They were seeing him for the first time. Most of the people knew the party and Karan Sharma, but they saw Vikram Rathore for the first time on stage.

"Thank you, Mister, for inviting me on the dais. Today, I, Vikram Rathore, the presenter of the party and speaker of the party, will speak in front of you people for the first time. I am really excited for today and really excited to show and present you the greatness of my party. I, Vikram Rathore, will address all the needed issues and I will tell you the solutions as well.

"Well, today we are going to talk about everything. Not a single topic but about everything. I can see today's ruling party is doing well. They are really good for those who can write dumb on their forehead - there was a huge sound wave from the public and Karan smiled - yes, I am not lying. I am standing in front of you and I am not lying. I believe that the ruling party is not ruling; they are having fun. They don't know what is going on here. They don't know what people need. They don't know what people are suffering from. They don't know what their state is up to. They just know what their close friends are up to. They just know what money is up to. The ruling party has won two consecutive elections and is ruling from the previous ten years, but I think, actually believe that they have just done nothing in these precious years. They have just had fun and spent money on nothing but corruption and false accusations.

"You know, some years ago, a big *Indian bank heist* was done. But do you think they have done something? They could not figure out the mastermind. They just cried like babies, bribed people, and then stopped everything. They don't know what development means. They don't know what people mean. They just know about money. Hey! We have a large amount of money, but we care for our people. We don't make rich people as our friends; we make people our friends. They don't know what people are saying. They don't know what people are demanding. They don't know the issues of electricity and water. They don't know about diseases that are common today. They have bribed smart doctors also. They have stopped the system. They have just done the fun they planned, but what about those fake promises."

"Now, I, Vikram Rathore, in front of everyone, promise you that we together will bring a revolution. That must be our personal motto. Our party is not a private organisation. We are not just a party. We are people. We are well-wishers. We are those who don't help people, but we sit with them to experience what they are going through and solve the problem together. Today, HIP is making a promise of transforming the state. If we transform the state, then surely in the future, we will transform the whole India. We, together, have to do the work. We together have to look for the problems. We have to respect the constitution. We have to follow it. Have we forgotten our fundamental duties? Of course not. We are here, together to solve the problems. We will bring a revolution. We will change the system. We have to turn ourselves modern. We have to be efficient. We have to be scientific. Stop believing in myths and stereotypes, just go for action. Save water now and then, see magic. You won't complain again about anything. To make it all happen, to make it all possible, follow HIP. We are your future. We will win and surely win because the whole India has to win. Thank you!"

There was the loudest applause ever. Karan had never heard such great applause or such a great speech. He was sure that this man was born to rule. He was just astonished. People went crazy. They were shouting, 'HIP zindabad,' and it was a proud moment for the party. Karan was really happy and excited for the future. Vikram was still on the dais, motivating people. He was crazy. He was mad. He was a legend.

❧

The other speeches ended, and the party had booked a whole hotel. Vikram and Karan were in one room. They were exhausted, but Vikram could feel his fire. His memories didn't seem to hurt him anymore. Anyways, his speech had such a great impact on people that Karan knew they had won a constituency. Not only had the people there listened to the speech, but the whole of India. There was media. Surely, it was more visible in the state only.

"That was great, Vikram," said Karan and appreciated him. "I never thought that you could be such a speaker. I thought you would pull the gun out and tell people to vote for the party or else!"

They both laughed hard. It was such a great day for them. They decided to stay in Lucknow for more functions and then move to Varanasi again.

They had their people set for the MLA positions. Vikram was going to be the mastermind of the party, and Karan the leader and future C.M.

Vikram's speech had highlighted many issues in public, like the great Indian bank heist. It was a great heist that took place in a bank in Uttar Pradesh. The mastermind had looted about 700 crores rupees and could not be found by the police. The case was closed, but after his speech, it was *revived*. It may cause great chaos in the future. Who was the *mastermind?* But talking of now, Karan was happy. They were smoking cigars. Vikram had a really good style of smoking than him.

"You smoke well," said Karan to Vikram when he was making shapes out of smoke.

"Just learned with experience," replied Vikram, and they both enjoyed the cigars. They seemed not to end, but they did, and they went to sleep. They had to prepare more programmes and people. For that, they needed time and efficiency. They had a year, and they had Vikram.

They woke up. They had to leave for Varanasi. They had a programme there and then many places. It was a never-ending process, but they had to do it for the sake of everything.

They left for Varanasi. They were moving through a village when some people stopped them. They seemed to be teenagers and they had bats with them. Their intentions seemed not to be good.

"HEY, STOP THE CAR!" shouted a boy, and they stopped. They were surprised. A bunch of boys stopping them, why?

"What is the matter?" asked the driver. But to their surprise, the boy hit the driver with a bat and left him unconscious. The people in the car were scared and shocked.

"What the hell, man!" shouted Karan.

The boys forced everyone out. They took the guns in their possession. Vikram was silent. The boys had just made them hostages.

"What is the matter, you people?" asked Karan in a terrible situation.

"You are those rich, shit people. You just make promises and do nothing!" said a boy. Vikram felt what the boy meant, and he knew that he was right.

"WHAT?" said Karan, "Are you MAD?"

"Yes, we are," said the boy in a miserable voice. "We are just worth nothing. You take the power and enjoy it."

"What are…"

"No, Karan!" interrupted Vikram. "They are not lying. They are telling the truth. Ministers make promises and do nothing. There is shame in that because all are shameless here!"

"What do you mean?" asked Karan angrily. "Are you saying that I am shameless?"

"Relax, my friend," said Vikram, "you are not a minister yet."

Karan raised his eyebrows and understood. The boys seemed simple, but then there came a big gang of gangsters. They were adults and were harmless. They pushed the little boys and took control.

"Hey, you sons of bitches!" said a fat man. "What the hell are you doing here?"

Vikram was on the urge to smack him down, but he controlled himself.

"We are politicians, listen, we can take you to jail!" replied Karan, and he knew that these words were of no use.

The fat man slapped him. Vikram still controlled himself. Karan was making exclamations of pain.

"Hey! Hey!" said Vikram calmly. "Stop. What are you doing?"

"Get lost, you bitch!" replied another man in anger.

"Stop!" said Vikram again calmly, and they believed that he is that nerd type of guy. "You should not fight."

"Listen," said one man, "Mr. Priest is here to give lessons!"

"I am no priest!" replied calm Vikram. "I am just telling you, and that is simple."

"Get lost, you motherfucker! You don't know anything. You piece of shit! Get LOST!" shouted a man. It was the line that he had crossed.

"FUCK OFF!" shouted Vikram and jumped on him.

He kicked him hard. He pressed his eyeballs. Everyone who came in between them, he smashed their faces. He showed no mercy. He was just brutally killing him, almost. It was scary to watch. He was punching his face and kicking his legs very hard. The fight was stopped somehow by everyone. Vikram was not stopping, but the other man was dragged out and the fight stopped.

"Hello, Vikram!" shouted Karan, surprised. "What the hell are you doing?"

"You saw how we just…"

"Stop! This is not the way!" interrupted Karan. "Why did you just beat him?"

"WHY DID HE JUST ABUSE ME?"

"Hell! NO!"

"What no!"

"You are going mad!"

"NO! I AIN'T GOIN' MAD!"

"YES YOU ARE!"

"Stop everyone!" interrupted Majid. He was somehow effective and stopped the quarrel.

"That son of a bitch showing his levels?" said Vikram in surprise.

"You should have left him!" replied Karan. "He would have died!"

"Wish he had!"

❧

They all reached Varanasi. It was beautiful there. They saw the Ganga. They saw the people. They saw the beauty and the vibe. It was just very refreshing. It was the best feeling you could get. The feelings were different. It was just like heaven for them. Vikram was relaxed. His wound on the arm had become fresh again. It was one of their regular fights. He waits until he thinks he is ready to fight. They reached Karan's house and they stepped out of the car.

"Relaxing," said Karan and Vikram in unison.

They both smiled and became happy. It was a huge mansion. It was like a *haveli* of old style but was royal and prestigious. Vikram smiled when he saw the same girl again with whom he met first. Vikram was wearing formal attire. He was looking dashing. He had a medium-sized beard, just like those gangsters. He had styled hair, sides trimmed and remaining upwards. He was dashing.

He could easily attract anyone, not until he is in a bad mood. He looked good but fierce also. Who knew that this man had already killed a dying man? He was still behaving well until he was fired by some incidents. They went inside and sat on the couches to relax a little bit.

There was a book lying by. It seemed interesting to Vikram. It was about the economy of India. He took the book and started reading it.

"You can read?" asked Karan in surprise.

"I told you, I am not a 10th pass, but that doesn't mean I haven't studied anything on my own. Class passing is just a school convention."

"No, I mean, you never read before me, so I was just shocked," said Karan in a normal tone.

"Yeah, I can read and write and do anything a person does," said Vikram in response.

"I did not mean to…"

"When did I say you meant," replied Vikram with a smiling face, "it is just my mistake."

"What is your mistake?" asked Karan with a tight eyebrows.

"My mistake was that I left my beautiful life for nothing but an undesired decision. Without thinking anything, my blood was getting hot and I just messed up my life. But that also didn't ruin my life. If I am here, it's just because of that decision, but being here is also a demerit of my decision. It is hard sometimes to think, but you have to think because you have to or you are just busted. You are forced. You are immature. You are nothing when compared to the outer world. If that day, I had remained patient, I would have been doing some good job and getting good money,"

"Yeah!" replied Karan even though he had not even understood his one word. He is just philosophical, thought Karan.

"You are shaped by your decisions. If your decision had been to go for civil services, you would have been living a different life, but life is already decided."

"Civil services? Huh!" said Karan in a sassy tone. "I don't even think about it."

"You could go for that, I guess," said Vikram in jest.

"No way!" replied Karan, "I am forty-five!"

"I see!" replied Vikram, 'You see, I had just opened the book and we reached Delhi for no reason!'

They both laughed hard. Vikram continued reading the book and noted some important points. He read about everything, from politics to the economy. He even revised some history as well. It gave a boost to his knowledge.

"Can I have some books related to finance?" demanded Vikram, while he was reading the book.

"That is the whole section," pointed Karan to a big wardrobe with no glass, just open (I don't know what it is called). It was huge. It had a sticker on top, 'Financial education'.

He searched through books and took some in his hands. That night he remained awake and learned the basics of financial education. When he opened his eyes, he found himself lying on the table. He opened his eyes and then went to the washroom. He bathed and became fresh.

"Vikram, you slept on the table!" said Karan and smiled at him as he moved towards the dining table for breakfast. He smiled back and made a seat for him.

He ate the breakfast. There were omelettes. There was wine, which he avoided and drank orange juice instead. He was amazed by this kind of breakfast.

Where are the *paranthas*? Where is the chicken? Where is the water? Where are the boiled eggs? Where are the almonds? Where are the *aloos*? Where is the breakfast?

These rich people just eat some spoiled eggs, juice, and wine and think they are superior, thought Vikram to himself.

He remembered the dream he had while sleeping that day. He saw his brother. He saw him hugging him. He saw his smile. He could feel his heartbeat. He was regretting his death.

He went back to the library and wrote a letter. There was the address of the temple. He wrote it there. He wasn't sure why he was writing this. Just because it would lighten up his heart.

Dear, brother,

I remember you. I remember the date. I remember what had happened. I remember the scenes. I remember the burial. I remember the blood. I remember my note on the wall. I hope you are all right. I don't know if you are there because I never saw you again. I buried my family, and I am sure that they are dead. But I always wish that you are alive. I haven't even touched a girl as you said in my childhood that they are toxic. But you were wrong. You are a liar. You met that Sneha Kapoor secretly and told me to stay away from girls. I don't mind you meeting anyone. Just come back. I want my blood family. I am fed up. Let me tell you I am here doing some politics. I have everything. I have money and whatever you want. Just come back. I had done a big crime years back just for something stupid, to let you know. I don't wanna make it a big thing, I just want you. If you are alive, then come and meet me. I still love you,

Yours truly,

Vicky!

He felt a tear in his left eye. He was emotional. He was crying. He just was. It was incredible. He could feel the pain. He remembered his past and felt numb for the first time since then. He remembered his mother, father, and all the other people, and then he remembered their dead faces. He was hopeless at that time.

He went to the post office. Then he submitted his letter and completed all the formalities. Then he came back and started preparing for future agendas and propaganda. He read many books. He read about India's past. He figured many things out.

He read about geography. He read about democracy. He read about diversity. He read the history. The history of Guptas, Mauryans, the Delhi Sultanate, the Mughals, and the British Raj. He was fascinated. He read about international history, or simply world history. He read the French Revolution, Russian Revolution, Nazis, world wars, the Cold War, UN, NATO, and all other things.

His best quality was that he remembered things quickly. Even though, in the topics, he could not remember all the dates and names, but all the other concepts were clear in his mind. He was reading all the other things as well. He had read many concepts in his childhood, but how come he could remember all that.

10

The Big Argument

"Vikram, I wanted to let you know that I have hired a new member for our party," said Karan while they were talking to each other about the party.

"Who?" asked Vikram in surprise.

"It is Sukhwinder Singh."

"Any background?" asked Vikram again.

"He worked at the rival party first, but then he left it because they were rubbish," replied Karan in vain.

"Who told you that?" asked Vikram to assure.

"Why are you being inquisitive?" asked Karan in turn.

"Just tell me, nah!"

"He told me, of course, who else could?"

"And you believed him?"

"Yes, he is a good guy,"

"Who told you that?"

"I know a person just by talking to him,"

"Do you think he really is?" asked Vikram.

"Yes!"

"Fine, but stay alert,"

"For what?" asked Karan, surprised.

"For your job and your position," he replied, normally.

"What do you mean?" asked Karan again.

"You can't trust anyone today, especially a person from the other party," he stated cautiously.

"Are you being jealous or what?"

"What the hell?" he wasn't expecting that from Karan.

"No, I mean you are behaving…"

"SHIT! Man, I never thought you'd think like that!" replied Vikram angrily. "You are trusting another person but not your own!"

"WHAT?" asked Karan. "My own? You are in my party because you said so, and I don't consider anyone my own!"

"Do you think that I am being mean by helping you?"

"No, you are not helping me! You are helping yourself,"

"Fuck, man! You are really being rude!" shouted Vikram very loudly.

"No, I am not! I prefer to trust one who I trust, not one who makes me trust him,"

"I don't care who you trust, but you can't let anyone be in our party,"

"*My* party," he said, and he was not making any eye contact.

"Fine, your party, but still think…"

"You don't teach me," this time he was forcing himself.

"I am not teaching you, I am just telling you,"

"You are being selfish. You are jealous of that man,"

"You are not trusting me, but that unknown man!"

"He is not unknown!"

"That means I am?" he was broken by the remarks.

"Maybe, as you think," he replied conceitedly.

"Man, I never thought my friend, like you, would ever just think like that!"

"What friend? Just partners,"

"Do you think that I am helping you for myself?"

"Yes, there is no alternative," replied Karan while looking somewhere else.

"You don't think all do this for symbiosis?"

"I don't care, I like that guy,"

"When I told him I hate him, I just told you to be alert,"

"That means you don't trust him?"

"I never met him,"

"But I have, and I know how he is,"

"Why are you making *raite ka pahad*? (Making a small thing a big argument)"

"It is not like that, I can sense," he said again in vain.

"Sense what?"

"What do you think?"

"What do I think?"

"Better not tell you,"

"Just tell nah!" asked Vikram in a friendly way, hoping for better results and to avoid a big argument.

"I told you, you are jealous. You think if someone else comes, he would take care of the party and I will lose the position and respect. The power I wanted is in danger and I will do whatever!"

"Shit man, I am leaving!" he made it final when he knew he couldn't handle it anymore.

"Leave, I don't care!"

Vikram left with Majid. Majid was confused as well as surprised. He could not understand anything.

"What is the matter, young man?"

"Nothing that son of a bitch thinks he is a god himself. He is nothing but a piece of shit,"

"What happened? Tell me."

"He hired some son of a bitch and threw me out because of him,"

"Why?"

"Like I know, he thinks that Singh is more trustworthy than this Singh,"

"That is wrong,"

"That is bullshit!"

"What are you thinking now?"

"What?"

"About the future?" said Majid brightly, but with something else in his heart.

"He will invite me himself!" said Vikram and smiled.

"How?" asked the confused white-bearded.

"Just watch and see,"

"Why will he?"

"He will, trust me."

It seemed odd for the old man to understand this. Why would he invite him again? That is again nonsense.

"That is not possible, I guess,"

"You guess, but I believe,"

"Do you believe that he will not let you come?"

"Dumb old man, I believe that he will let me into his party again,"

"But how?"

"Again, same question!"

"But you are not giving any reply,"

"I ain't?"

"Yes!"

"But that is, again, wrong. I told you to watch,"

"What have you done now?"

"Something that will let him come to me!"

"Do you really believe?"

"You piece of shit! How many times have I told you?"

They left for their house. They reached there. The journey was not comfortable. Their car was making much noise. They entered the house and relaxed on the sofa.

"That car is just hell!"

"Yeah!" replied the old man nonchalantly.

"I need to change it,"

"What are you going to buy?"

"What do you think, G-Wagon or Rolls Royce?"

"Whichever is damn good!"

"I dreamed of having both,"

"Then buy both."

"Yes, that is a good idea!"

❧

They had done the car deal. They bought a G-Wagon instantly, but the Rolls Royce was a challenge. It wouldn't come instantly.

"Sir, I told you, it will take up to a year," said a man on the phone. He was the manager of Rolls Royce somewhere. He knew it takes less time but he did not want to argue and end it up with a little green.

"I will pay you extra!" bribed Vikram.

"How much?" another man of appetite replied.

"What do you think?" Vikram gave him leverage.

"Whatever suits you!" he said with a bright mood, which Vikram could feel in his voice.

"I will pay extra for the crore,"

"A bit more, can you?"

"I will pay an extra 5 crores, done?"

"Obviously, sir!"

"Now how much time will it take?"

"Not much, just 8 months!"

"Fuck you!"

❧

They were now discussing their own work. They were not sure whether to continue their own party.

"What do you think?" asked the old man.

"No!"

"Why?"

"I told you, he will invite us to his party," he said, annoying the old man.

"Then what shall we do till then?"

"Wait! What can we even do?"

They switched on the TV. They saw some news. It was boring at first. They put on that *taaza khabar*, top-hundred news.

They changed the channel and saw something they never expected.

"People in this village are dying of hunger and thirst. There is no water. Some days ago, two small children died. Their parents could not even afford the funeral. Because they don't have any money. There is no concept of electricity. What development is this? Small children are dying for no reason. This is hell.

"Government is spending money on some useless things whereas these innocent people don't have the right to life. The government is trying their best but why can't they do this. This is just one village; there are thousands of such places where there is nothing. Here you can see the visuals - the photos were of small children. Their bones were sticking out. People were as thin as a stick. The village was just desolation. It was hell - if you cannot even feel for them, then you are no human!" These were the words of a reporter.

Vikram felt some urge. He realised something. He bought a car or two cars worth crores, and there, they can't even have a small meal.

"Is this revolution you wanted, Mister Vikram Rathore? You thought about changing India, but you can't even change a single person's life. You were deeply in money, politics, and power. But what about other people? They don't have anything. You have everything. This is shit. Why can't you just be the one who you wanted to be?" thought Vikram to himself.

He left the room and went to the washroom. He saw himself in the mirror. His face. He was fine. He took off his shirt. He had a healthy body. He took off his pants. He was really healthy but what about those innocent weak people? What will they do? They have nothing. You are nothing, Vikram. You are nothing.

"It is the time, Vikram Rathore. It is the time that awaited you. It is the time for some action. Do what you wanted to do. You are not stone-hearted. You don't have your family, but you have yourself. Others have their family, but they can't even support them. You have to do what you have to do. You are surely not an angel from God or some chosen one. You are the one who has promised himself to be not less than a chosen one. It is your land. These are your family members. Forget what you said, 'good people are my family', then why are you leaving your family like this."

"You are nothing if you cannot do anything. Vikram Rathore, you have to bring about a revolution. You are the legend. You are the saviour. You have to do it. Do it now. You have money, and use the money to buy happiness and trust, not materialistic things. You have to change. I promise myself, even if I die, I have to bring a revolution. I have to promise myself whatever happens, whatever kills me, I don't care, I have to care for my people, if no one else can." He again thought to himself.

He was crying hard. The bathroom was soundproof. He shouted hard. He cried. He cursed himself. It was not the reporter who motivated him, it was his time, and it was he who had made a promise. His mother's promise. He had to do it. He remembered his cursed past. He promised that he would not let that happen again now or ever after; he had to change everything. Fuck money, fuck power, fuck politics, and fuck riches. He wanted a revolution, the biggest one ever!

PART 4

11

The Revolution Starts

The revolution starts. Yes, it does. The sparkle had changed into fire. He was on. He had forgotten everything in his past. Now, his ambition was just one, and he wanted to live for that. If not the whole world, then India. If not the whole India, then some states. If not some states, then one state. If not one state, then one city. If not one city, then one village. If not one village, then one family. If not one family, then just one person. He wanted to bring a revolution, even if it is just for one person.

He left the washroom and then met Majid.

"What happened, young man?" asked Majid when he saw his dull face.

"A lot happened."

"What lot?" asked Majid in confusion.

"I am leaving,"

"Where?" replied Majid in question.

"To my people,"

He went out at night. He had some cigars in his pocket. He went inside, cut one at the front, and lit it. Then he went out again.

He wanted some fresh night air. He smoked the cigar. It made him feel calmer. He thought about the dying people. The cigar was of no use. He felt heavy at that time. The visuals he had seen had disturbed him.

He was thinking about that when he found out something. He decided to make a team, a secret one. The members will be throughout the country. They won't show their identity and help people, even if they have to choose violence. He knew that the government would be against him, but he was ready. He had already promised that even if anything kills him in between his journey, he will not care, even if it is the government. But then he thought about from where he would make the team. Then he also got an idea. In a state, the number of constituencies, the number of people there. One person for one constituency. He had even named his gang (gang because it is going to do things illegally), 'The Legend's Club'. He was ready to set out. He was ready to go to every constituency of India, rather all states. He will find out one person, and that person will handle the other people. That person will choose the people for the constituencies. The person chosen by Vikram will be responsible for the state. Vikram himself was going to take control of UP.

Simply, he was creating his own government. Not a small one, but state and central both. It was challenging, but he was going to do it. His government was going to be more effective, responsible, and active. No elections, but still the best of all. The man was ready to create history and a place in people's hearts. Even if to save one person on the team, he would give his own life. It was his ambition. He could think of nothing but developing India. The concepts that children are taught in classes will be implemented in real life. This work was going to be done by none other than The Legends Club.

Now, he had to begin the work. He had to choose or he had to find people like him, who are willing to choose peace and make India as it never was. He had decided that they will kill all the criminals. That is, again, the main reason that the government will be after them because this is illegal.

It was midnight, and he was gazing at the stars. They looked incredible. Incredibly beautiful. He believed in his childhood that these stars were the dead people. But then, yes, he studied science and everything was clear.

He was thinking of The Legend's Club. He thought that he would go to the main states first. He decided that the first state would be Gujarat. He knew that his journey was going to be long, so it would take time, but he was ready. His fire was at its peak. He was burning.

Suddenly, this emergence of a childhood dream was abnormal, but it just was. He didn't care why and how; he just cared about yes.

He went inside. He took out the beer. He shook the bottle hard and then started drinking it. He felt dizzy but didn't stop drinking. While he was drinking, he fell down on the marble floor. Suddenly, memory flashes were coming in front of him. He could see his dead family.

Blood. Screams. Gunshots. Swords. Deaths. Revenge. Arshid Ahmad. The jail. The bank. The gunshots. The meeting. Abdul Majid. Politics. Karan Sharma. Fight. TV. Beer. He was frustrated.

He didn't want to wait. He decided that he would move to Gujarat the next day. But then he questioned himself, why Gujarat?

Charity begins at home. He wanted to create a fully-fledged government at UP first. He had to face the chosen government. He had to face the police. But he wanted to win the hearts of the people. He didn't want to go for politics again. He wanted to create politics.

He knew he wasn't born to do what everyone is doing. He was born for something new. He was born for the greatest cause of the *Indian Revolution*, and he will be doing that as soon as possible. He had to go to every main city for one person. He will be starting that the next day. He wanted to choose Varanasi first. He was confused. But then it struck him, and he chose Abdul Majid for Varanasi. After all, he used his name Banarasi.

He chose to go to Lucknow, the city of *nawabs*. He opened his mobile and bought an emergency ticket to Lucknow. It cost him a lot, but he was well-off after all. He then, without sleep, went to Abdul Majid and interrupted his dreams.

"Majid, stand up," said Vikram in a hurried voice.

Majid who was half-awake by then found it odd. He usually didn't call him by his name, but when he does, there is something wrong.

"What is the matter, Vicky?" asked Majid in a sleepy voice.

"There is something important for you, wake up." said Vikram and pushed him abruptly. Unintentionally, but with force, he woke up and sat on the bed with one eye closed and one open for the sake of listening.

"What is it?" asked Majid, who was now almost fine to talk.

He told him everything. From his childhood to now. He had lied about his life. He had told him that he never went to the temple. Rather, he was out of the temple when all that happened. Majid was amazed as well as shocked. He knew everything now. He felt some different energy in Vikram. He felt royalty in him. He was there to support him. He would do it for him. Even if he dies. These fast decisions are made. They are not unrealistic. When something strikes, it strikes.

"Fine, dear, I am ready," said Majid to Vikram in a calm voice. "I am here ready to take over Banaras."

"That's done, and I am moving to Lucknow, so be alert."

"Passengers, please tighten your seat belts and get ready as we are moving to Lucknow. The plane is ready to take off…"

Vikram was on the flight. It wasn't his first time on a plane, but he also wasn't eager for planes. He was fond of cars.

"Hell, these airplanes are hell!" said the woman who was near his seat, actually next to him.

"Yes," replied Vikram just because he wanted to say that, "they just take the hell out of a person."

"That is so true." said the girl and opened her purse. She had some makeup in it, and then she did what Vikram had thought. What else could she do?

"Are you from Lucknow?" asked Vikram with great curiosity.

"Yes, and you?" asked the girl.

"I am from," said Vikram with a pause, "India."

"Ah!" remarked the girl, "Actually, I was asking about a particular place."

"Well, right now, I am from Banaras," replied Vikram when nothing else came to his mind.

"Beautiful place, isn't it?" asked the girl even though she knew but she wanted to create a conversation with the guy.

"Well, if you ask me," said Vikram and smiled, "it is."

He said in a tone like only he lived in Varanasi. The girl seemed interested in him.

"So, your family?" she asked.

"Well," replied Vikram and took a long pause, "I just don't have any blood-related people alive, but I have a large family."

"So sorry!" she exclaimed when she heard him.

"Why are you apologising?" asked Vikram, "It isn't your mistake at all."

"What killed your parents or relatives, I don't know actually?"

"They died in a massacre actually just because of one person,"

"Where is that person?"

"He lives with me."

❧

They were in deep conversation. Vikram also liked talking with her.

"Sorry, I forgot what you do?" asked the girl.

"For what purpose do you work?" asked Vikram in reply.

"Me?" asked the girl.

"No, not you, I am talking generally," said Vikram, while the 'you' referred to people.

"Money, I guess,"

"Yes, and I have lots of."

The girl smiled and covered her mouth, as she was shy. Why was she shy? She was really interested.

"How much money?" asked the girl.

"How much do you need?"

Again, she smiled and hit Vikram on the arm. Vikram smiled and hit her back gently.

"Well, you forgot the main thing." said Vikram when he remembered.

"What? Makeup?" asked the girl in a hurry.

"Hmm! So silly of you, you didn't even tell me your name."

"Sorry! I am Maisha, and you?"

"I am Vikram," replied Vikram proudly, "Vikram Rathore."

"Heavy name."

"Cute name."

The girl again smiled and pulled Vikram's cheek as if she would tear him up, but the main thing was that…

"I like you." said the girl shyly and covered her mouth.

"Well, in that case, I love you."

They were both silent for a long time. The plane landed. They were off. They were in the airport, and then Vikram finally broke the silence.

"What do you do?"

"I?" said Maisha. "I am a journalist, by the way."

Why does every main character of a story always meet up with a journalist?

"Where are you going in Lucknow?" added Maisha.

"Nowhere, just looking for a place, maybe a hotel,"

"You can stay at my house," said the girl, "if you want."

"Actually, I don't want to trouble you, but you can always give me your number."

She smiled again, a smiley woman, and gave him her phone number. He saved her number and named her "TMCGE". That was odd.

"What is that?" asked Maisha when she saw the name.

"The cutest girl ever!" replied Vikram and winked at her.

She smiled and went away. Were they in love? Fell in love on an airplane? Was Vikram going mad?

Vikram then booked a hotel. It was a grand hotel. 20,000 rupees per night. Pretty expensive for the middle class.

He was thinking how to find the right guy. Before going to sleep, he called Maisha.

"Hi!" said Maisha, "Can you do one thing, text me!"

Without any further ado, she ended the call. Vikram was amazed, but there is texting after all.

Vikram: Hi!

Beautyqueenmaisha: Hi

Vikram was amazed after seeing her name. Beauty queen? That was odd, but it wasn't a lie. She really was beautiful.

Vikram: How r u?

Beautyqueenmaisha: Just doin' well. Actually, my parents are here so I can't talk on the phone.

Vikram: Are you alone this time?

Beautyqueenmaisha: No, my parents are just here.

Vikram: So what do you do as a journalist?

Beautyqueenmaisha: Just research and write about the Indian economy.

Vikram thought she was a quite good person.

Vikram: That is good!

Beautyqueenmaisha: I know! Haha.

Vikram: Can you work with me?

Beautyqueenmaisha: What work?

Vikram: I am making a team all over India. I want you for Lucknow.

Beautyqueenmaisha: What is the work?

Vikram: We have to make India developed and peaceful.

Beautyqueenmaisha: Well.

She didn't message further. Vikram thought that she wouldn't talk to him anymore. But after some time, he got her call.

"Why didn't you answer me?" asked Vikram.

"Actually, I want to meet you!" she said enthusiastically.

"Where?" he asked in confusion.

"Where are you right now?"

"I am at a hotel," he replied hopefully.

"Which hotel?" she asked like a usual journalist.

"Near that big bazaar,"

"Oh! Royal Dessert,"

"Yeah, whatever!" he replied and found it quite odd to remember names of hotels just because they were good.

"I am meeting you there tomorrow,"

"But…" she had cut the call. It was disappointing but a happy moment as well. He was excited to meet her. He was impatient to meet her.

She was beautiful. She had long, thin, smooth, and silky hair. She had a cute nose, and her eyes were incredibly attractive. She was like those beautiful actresses in ads, but she was more than them. She was almost five feet and some inches tall. She had a beautiful body. She was very cute. Vikram couldn't stop thinking about her.

It was the next day. She had already reached the destination. But Vikram was ready. He seemed to have been ready for ages.

"Hi!" she squealed and hugged him tight. He was amazed as well as happy.

"Hi! Come sit,"

"Tell me all about your work!"

"Well, promise you won't tell anyone!"

She seemed a bit sad but was ready.

"Ok, promise, tell me now!"

Vikram told him everything. It took him almost two hours. He started from his childhood to teenage to now. Everything, he explained crisply. She seemed more interested. She was sad as well as empathetic towards him.

They moved on the bed. Vikram became silent. Maisha also did not talk. She slowly held his hand in her own. Vikram could feel a flow of sudden energy. She was touching him very erotically. Slowly she put his hand on her belly, and then pressed it. Vikram did not move. He felt very hard and was feeling uncontrolled. She then slowly took his hand to her breasts. Vikram, at that time, used his hand on his own. He touched it and became lost. He was doing it for the first time and his excitement made his heart beat very fast.

"How is it?" asked Maisha with a very low tone of voice.

"Incredible!" he replied, also in a very low tone but slowly.

He slowly turned to her. His hand was on her breast. He removed his hand and tried to open her shirt. He was unbuttoning it.

She closed her eyes and bit her lips. Vikram was full of energy. He threw the shirt sideways. Then he put his hand on her back. He opened her bra. It took him a while. Then he could see her breasts, fully naked. He was very excited and made some odd positions. He pressed them. He used his mouth and held both her hands in his one hand and touched her leg with hers.

She, after that, opened his shirt, which she easily could do. She kept it on the side table. Then she unbuttoned her pants. She then had just her underwear on. Vikram took off his underwear. Then he was fully nude. They touched each other. First Vikram touched and she seemed a bit scared, but then merged like a tide merges back with the ocean.

She touched him. And he touched her everywhere. He opened her underwear. They were both nude. They could feel each other's bodies. She was soft, very soft. They kissed. For a long time, they were intimately touching each other and kissing. He started touching her clitoris. She moaned.

He jumped on her. Then they were one. They were on the bed. She couldn't control anything. She was moaning and just moaning.

Vikram, after half an hour, was about to end. He took his penis out. Then she rubbed her hand against it. She used his hands, breasts, and mouth for long pleasure. After some time, they were done.

❧

"It was fun!" she said after everything was normal.

"Yes, surely it was!" replied excited Vikram, who didn't know what to reply and felt odd.

"Have you ever been with any girl before?" she asked to confirm the scene.

"Never in my life have I just worked for whatever!"

She was happy. She seemed glowing. She was deeply in love with him.

"I love you so much!"

"I love you more than you!"

"Not possible!"

They laughed and lay on the bed, stretching themselves.

"I don't know in how much time I just liked you. Yesterday we were strangers and today, one!"

Vikram nodded. He was also happy. He was really excited, very much. For the first time in his life, a girl was there for him. Great!

They talked about work. They were really close to each other now. There was no way she could lose him ever, and vice versa. They were in really deep love. They felt kind of odd without each other. This feeling just emerged within minutes. It was a miracle. But she was his work partner now. They discussed The Legends Club.

"I Guess it is time to create The Legends Club!"

"Yes, let's go!"

12

The Legends Club

They had made an ambition. She was so much into him that she gave up her dream and decided to work for him. God knows why she was so close to him. They loved each other after all. It was a great experience. They had empathy for each other. Lucknow and Varanasi were set. Now they had to move forward. Vikram gave the work to Maisha to look after all the other places.

She was given the task of choosing representatives of many places like Bareilly, Ahmedabad, Aligarh, Mirzapur, etc.

Vikram decided to move to Gujarat. He booked a ticket and went to Gujarat. In order to avoid meeting anyone on the plane like the previous time, he slept. When the plane landed, he went to the main airport calmly. He was wearing a hoodie and shorts. He had sunglasses and headphones around his neck. Then he booked a hotel and took a taxi to the hotel.

"Hi, sir. Where do you want to go?" asked the driver when Vikram signalled him to stop.

"I want to go to Pearl Soft Hotels," replied Vikram in a calm tone.

"Ok, sir, sit. I will take you," replied the driver innocently.

The driver seemed innocent (I know, he said innocently, so he is innocent!). He drove slowly, but he seemed tense.

"What happened, bhai? What is the matter?" asked Vikram in a caring voice.

"Nothing, sir, just those stereotypical, age-old problems," replied the driver. He seemed to be around twenty-five. Pretty young to drive a cab.

"Just tell me, maybe I can help you!" said Vikram and smiled.

"What help will you provide, sir? It is a matter of money, after all," said the driver and smiled. He hid the pain he had inside him.

"How much do you earn?" asked Vikram curiously.

"Around twenty thousand rupees a month," replied the driver and again gave a painful smile.

"Do you think India needs a revolution?" asked Vikram.

"Sir, revolution? Yes, it does. We need to change the economic system. We have to look forward. Even if it takes sacrifices, we should be ready. India needs to be better after all," replied the driver confidently.

"Have you studied?" asked Vikram.

"Sir, I have a master's in economics, but this unemployment in India crushes even the most brilliant of minds!"

"What will be your reaction, if I tell you that I can pay you a lakh a month?" asked Vikram.

The driver stopped the car with a jerk.

"What is the work, sir?" asked the driver enthusiastically.

"We need to change India!"

The driver accepted when Vikram told him his plan.

"Sir, but what about my family?" asked the driver with a sad mood.

"Don't worry, they will be safe!"

"Then it is fine, sir. I will create a team, The Legend's Club of Gujarat!"

"That's my boy!"

Gujarat was done. These unexpected meetings led him to meet very good and broad-minded people. Thank God, he wasn't a journalist.

Then he came back to Varanasi. Majid and Maisha were there. He told them, and they were happy. Now they discussed the next state, Punjab. The state of *everything* had the next turn. Vikram had taken the phone number of the man from Gujarat. His name was Virat. He had managed to find two more people. In UP, Ahmedabad, Aligarh, and Mirzapur were done. They needed more people, and they believed that they would find more people.

Vikram took the flight to Amritsar. It was a very vibrant city, full of joy, but sometimes these people get so angry that they don't spare the other one. That was different; normally Punjabis were the most brilliant of all. He first went to the Golden Temple. Then he visited Jallianwala Bagh.

Jallianwala Bagh was the place where General Dyer had ordered his troops to shoot the people there. They were holding a peaceful protest against the arrest of two important figures. But Dyer showed no mercy and killed hundreds, and thousands were wounded. Some people even jumped into the very big well. It is very deep. But after that, Sardar Udham Singh went to London and killed Dyer in public. That is just a part of history, and Vikram was proud that he knew this. He even saw the memorials of Sardar Udham Singh. He saw the bullet marks. It made him feel tickly. He felt odd there. The place where thousands were suffering, people came to enjoy there. It all happened on 13 April 1919, the dreaded day. It made him remember another dreaded day.

However, Vikram saw all this and went to a hotel, a local one, nearby. In the hotel, he paid and completed all the formalities. He spent the night there. He chatted with Maisha and felt happy. Now the main task was to find a trustworthy person. But before that, he called Virat. He said that he was finding people. Vikram had also paid him five lakhs in advance.

It was the next day when the hunt began. He woke up, got fresh, and made some breakfast. He ate some kulche with butter, enough to make him what we call a *healthy* person.

He felt energetic. He then went out. He took a taxi, but the driver seemed not to be interested in any revolution or whatever there was.

Then he went to the Golden Temple again. He saw many people. He prayed to God for help. Then he went out. He ate some ice cream and cotton candy. However big a person gets in terms of age, that immaturity is still there. That childish soul is still there, ready to play and shout.

He was walking through a narrow *gali* when a biker came fast and hit his ice cream.

"Hey Behenchod!" shouted Vikram angrily after the biker passed by.

The biker stopped. He stopped at the main road. Vikram walked quickly towards him in anger. He reached him.

"What the hell do you think…" said Vikram but stopped when he saw a gun in the biker's hand. Vikram was confused. Why did all the Punjabis have guns? He thought that almost more than half of all the weapons resided in Punjab.

"What were you saying?" asked the biker in vain.

"I was saying, will you want some more expensive ice cream? Actually, this is cheap!"

"Hmm!" said the biker, "give me your mother's phone number so that I can talk to…"

This was the greatest punch he had ever used. The biker flew in the air. The bike dropped on the ground. The biker stood up. He took his knife and tried to hit him. But to his surprise, Vikram took out a brand new Desert Eagle.

"Sir, do you want some ice cream?"

Vikram reached a chemist. He went inside.

"What do you want, sir?" asked the chemist cheerfully.

"I want nothing. Focus on your work," said someone to the right of Vikram.

"Sir, I was talking to this gentleman," explained the chemist.

"OH! Sorry, I am really sorry. I am just frustrated with this system. You see a minister just killed someone with his car. Why are they ministers? They have power and they think justice is a joke. India actually needs a revolution!" said the man while looking into his phone.

"Sir?" asked Vikram.

"Yes," replied the man.

"I wanted to talk to you if you don't feel bad," said Vikram, and the man nodded.

"What did you actually want to buy, sir?" asked the chemist to Vikram.

"I wanted some babies, are they here?" joked Vikram and the other man smiled.

They were outside. Vikram took him into a big hotel.

"Do you want to kidnap me?" asked the man.

"No, sir, not exactly," said Vikram. "What do you do for a living and to raise your family?"

Vikram asked because the man seemed to be a bit older. He looked around forty.

"Well, I have no job and no family!" replied the man in regret.

Vikram closed his eyes, regretting his question, but he wanted to change the mood.

"Do you want to change India?" asked Vikram when they finally reached their hotel room.

"Of course, but I can't stand politics," said the man.

"What is your name, sir?" asked Vikram.

"I am Sukhwinder Singh," replied the man. Vikram remembered that he had heard this name somewhere. Then it struck him. It was the name of the dreaded man who wanted to work for Karan. He didn't want to think about him.

"Have you ever been in politics?" asked Vikram curiously to make it clear.

"NO! NEVER! Not my cup of tea," replied the man and smiled.

"Sir, will you work for India? You will get paid as well. All you have to do is make up a team in Punjab, coordinate, vanish every crime, and help benefitting other common people. It is actually our own government. You want money, I will give you. You just have to make Punjab anew. You have to develop this. There is danger. Police and government will be after you. So you have to do it secretly!" said Vikram. He told him everything about the ambition and past and vision; it inspired the old man.

The man nodded and thought about something.

"Exactly as our legends did against Angrez Raj for independence," said the man, confirming in a Punjabi accent.

This was the best example Vikram had ever heard of.

"Yes, exactly!" replied Vikram proudly.

"I am ready to do everything for my Punjab and India!"

❧

Vikram reached Varanasi again. He had told them everything. Three states done. Majid and Maisha heard this and became happy.

Maisha had left her family. After Vikram told her to tell him the reason, she said she said some excuses and unbelievable things.

It seemed simple as the way she told but exactly more difficult. She handled life like a piece of butter, her talent, maybe.

Vikram informed Virat about it. He had also found many people. Sukhwinder also knew about Virat and was happy. They knew that whole India must be controlled.

Vikram wanted a break. He wanted to completely take over these three states first.

He informed everyone in the team. Virat and Sukhwinder got 2 crores in their account. He told them to help people first. Getting rid of gangsters was a job for later.

Now was the turn to check if the magic worked. Vikram was ready to take over Uttar Pradesh first.

He decided to look at famous places first. He decided to help poor people. He wanted to give them food and shelter. This was not for money or power; it was because he wanted to. He went with his team, Maisha and Majid. They helped him. Majid considered her his daughter. He never had a daughter, but he had got one.

He went to every gully in Varanasi. He found that there were many people sitting on footpaths, begging for money. He gave everyone money there.

"May God bless you, *beta*," said one old woman when he gave her some food and money.

"Thanks *maaji*, I am going to buy you a house too!" replied Vikram. She smiled and gave him her blessings.

Everyone was getting food and money, but the main problem was a house. They didn't have a proper house to live in. They slept on the road, some even on benches. This was unbearable. How can someone not help them? He had to find land, plenty of land. Not only in Varanasi but in the whole of India. It seemed pretty impossible but still. He wanted to get land, by any means possible.

❧

"What do you think?" asked Majid to Vikram when they were talking about land.

"Well, we can see that later as well; we should nourish them. And yes! We should not forget other people also. The majority of people have land and a house but no money," said Maisha.

"That is also right!" replied Vikram, "We should first nourish every family."

"That is also right. What about Gujarat and Punjab?" asked Majid.

"I told them they are doing the same," replied Vikram proudly. His hope in them was really high.

"What about credits?" asked Majid worriedly.

"Don't worry, every person who is getting food and money also gets a poster, that is about me and our club," replied Vikram in vain, thinking he is great about these things. Taking credit was a skill he knew and had used many times in the past.

"When will we go to other states?" asked Maisha.

"We will first do these states and then look forward," replied Vikram. It was night already. They decided to sleep. Vikram and Maisha slept together.

In Punjab, Vikram was praised. Sukhwinder was doing his work very well. He knew that helping India prosper is not a bad thing to do. He helped many people. He had even bought many houses on sale for many people. Different people lived together. They were happy; after all, they had a home. They just wanted to see Vikram, not because he helped them but because he helped them with no intention of elections, vote or power. He was doing it for their benefit. Sukhwinder was also happy because he was getting a lot of praise. But he was confused about Vikram's money. The same was the case in Gujarat. He did not seem to work actively. He did not help many people. He seemed to have a problem.

They had ordered so much food, not for themselves but for the people, of course. They enjoyed the food when they ate with them in the streets and talked about the miseries of life.

Now, it was time to move to other places. Slowly he went to all places. Found representatives. He gave food and money to people.

But still houses were pending. It was UP and land is not available there like Punjab. The population is booming in UP and houses are rapidly growing, so land is also scarce.

"I have an idea," said Majid.

"What is it?" asked Vikram, hopefully hoping for some good plan.

"What if we somehow trap factory owners who have illegal work and drugs and take their factories? It is a lot of land. We will diminish the factories and start constructing houses there?"

Vikram was really impressed by the idea. He wanted to do it, but in some other way.

"We will not prove them wrong, but we will warn them and throw them out!" said Vikram and smiled to himself.

"But they can go to the police," said Majid tensely. He didn't want the police in between. He wanted to do things legally.

"Don't worry about the police, Karan will look after it!" said Vikram and surprised Majid.

"What? But how?" asked Majid in a surprised voice.

"Didn't I tell you?"

❧

"I told you a long time ago, old man. I told you he will not trap us, but I will trap him. He threw me out but forgot one thing; he had made a big mistake by believing in me. Not because I am not worthy, but because he is not worthy. When we were doing that concert or whatever it is called in Lucknow, I had taken 200 crores from him. He ain't leaving me without them. They are safe, but that doesn't mean I am going to give them back immediately!" said Vikram, who was conceited at that time.

Majid was impressed; rather, he was shocked at first.

"But how did you know he would throw you out?" asked Majid curiously.

"I didn't know it!" replied Vikram.

"Then how, why did you take money and what was the need at that time?" asked Majid, who was still looking for an answer because he wouldn't believe him.

"I will tell you sometime later, old man," replied Vikram. This was really an impressive moment. Majid was out of his wits.

"When did you talk with him last?" asked Majid.

"Just months ago, when we were at Mirzapur!" replied Vikram.

UP was logically his. People were craving for him. He now wanted to clear factories for two reasons. 1) He wanted land for houses. 2) He wanted UP pollution less.

"Hello, who is this?" asked a man from the phone. Vikram had called a businessman who had a large factory. The factory was located on around 100 acres of land.

"I am Vikram Rathore," replied Vikram.

"What do you want?" asked the man.

"I want your factory," said Vikram, thinking and waiting for some other answer. He was shocked.

"I actually wanted to sell it. I want just 77 crores for my land and factory," said the man. Vikram gulped and thought about it.

"Why do you want to sell?" asked Vikram. "Is the land illegal, or is the factory producing illegal things?"

"HEY! Don't you dare move to the police!" said the man in an angry voice.

"I won't move to the police, but the police always move to me, brother!" replied Vikram proudly and conceitedly.

"Who are you?" asked the man in an irksome voice.

"I told you, brother. I will bust you and you wont even know" he replied, taunting him.

"Behave, man. Who are you?" asked the man again.

"I told you, nah! I am Vikram Rathore!" he again replied with a sense of being powerful.

"Vikram Rathore, who?" he asked again.

"Listen, I am gonna blow up your factory and take the land. I ain't lying!"

"What do you want, listen, I *can* give you?" asked the man in a scared manner.

"I want land, just land or if you can give plenty of houses, that will also work," replied Vikram.

The man sighed on the phone and said, "Then you don't want any part of cocaine… fuck!"

"From what?" asked Vikram with high hopes.

"SHIT!" he exclaimed in regret.

"FROM WHAT, BITCH!"

"Fine! I am running a cocaine business and I thought you were after that," he said and then regretted his slipping tongue.

Vikram grinned to himself and found another fish for the trap. He knew that fate was with him because he wasn't doing anything wrong.

"Well, now I want," replied Vikram, "how much do you produce? Wait, meet me at your factory tomorrow at ten a.m."

The man agreed, and the phone call was done. Sometimes, people get out of control and tell their secrets. This is an example of a person who is not responsible and active. However, this was beneficial for Vikram.

"Why did you ask about cocaine?" asked Majid in a hurried voice.

"Listen, I found something," said Vikram. "We don't need to trap or warn. We can just buy the factories. But for that, we need more money. We can get a lot from cocaine. That bitch might be selling that in India, but I will sell it out of the country for more money!"

"That is hell risky!"

"I know, but don't tell Maisha anything."

Suddenly, Maisha came inside. She had a plate full of tea cups.

"What were you doing?" asked Maisha. She seemed to know nothing. They thought that she heard them.

"Nothing! Just work and all about Punjab!" replied Vikram.

"What in Punjab?" asked Maisha.

"The work there is going well!"

"What about Gujarat?" asked Maisha again.

"Hell! We don't have any news from Gujarat!"

"Call Virat!" said Majid quickly and in an odd way.

Vikram dialled his number, but he wasn't answering. After some time, the phone went switched off.

"There is some problem!" said Maisha in a more worried voice. Vikram felt confused and heavy-hearted for a reason.

"Vikram, move to Gujarat as soon as possible!"

"I am going tomorrow!"

❧

Vikram was on the plane. He was confused about how many times he had been on a plane since the first time he met Maisha. That was just an unexpected meeting. He never wanted to meet any girl, and after Maisha, he doesn't want to meet any other girl.

The plane was ready to take off. This time the voice, usual one, was in Hindi.

"Sabhi yaatri kripya dyaan de, vimaan udne ja raha hai. Kripya apni seatbelt laga le aur apne mobile switch off ya phir airplane mode

mai daal de. Dhanyewaad! (All the passengers, please take note! The plane is ready for takeoff. So, please switch off your phones or put them in airplane mode. And put on your seatbelts, thank you!)" said the speaker.

She was a lady. Vikram felt comfort after he got the usual training of plane things and conventions, and then the plane took off. The plane was in the air. The weather was unusual. Those black clouds and some thundering, same as shown in movies. The plane was very good. There were small TVs on all the seats. It was unusual that it had actually good movies on it. Vikram was watching some new romantic movie. Not that much erotic but more erotic than what he had seen till his life for fun. He was watching it when he got bored and turned on some Hollywood movies. He was astonished after seeing the kisses and all that romance.

"How's that possible?" asked Vikram to himself. He was amazed to see them kissing and being nude, either fully or half in front of everyone. That was odd for him. It wasn't usual in India.

He was watching the movie keenly. Nothing could stop him from watching more romantic scenes. He was amazed when he saw a couple engaging in sex alone on the bed. He wondered how they dared to do this when they knew it was going to be watched by everyone. The movie was 18+, and he was proud and happy that he was older than that. Everything was going fine until sometime.

"Sabhi yaatri kripya dyaan de. Mausam theek na hone ki wajah se hum Bhopal Airport par land karne wale hain, Dhanyewaad!" (All the passengers please listen carefully. Due to bad weather, we are going to land at Bhopal Airport. Thank you!)" said the speaker, again the same girl.

"Hell!" said Vikram.

"*Hum Mausam theek hone ke baad, Ahmedabad mein land karenge.* (WE WILL LAND IN AHMEDABAD, AFTER THE WEATHER IS FINE)." added the speaker.

"God! Her voice is sexy!" thought Vikram to himself.

They landed in Bhopal. He was worried because Virat was out of communication. It was odd. He had not expected this. Was Gujarat going to be out of control?

It was difficult to imagine. What about Virat's family? Was he facing any problems? Was he fed up with this idea? Was he killed? Nothing could be said.

Vikram had reached inside the airport. He took some tea and sandwiches. He felt uneasy inside. He called Maisha.

"Hello!" said Maisha excitedly on the phone, "Have you reached Gujarat?"

"We are in Bhopal!" replied Vikram and sighed. He was fed up.

"Why?" she asked in surprise.

"This fucking weather!" he replied with anger. He was frustrated and needed rest, but at the same time, he was restless.

"Ok! Calm down, honey!" she said adorably from the phone. This was the first time she called him honey; maybe he was a bee. He was grinning from the inside.

"Thank you, honey!" he replied and muted his speaker because he squealed due to excitement.

"Oooh!" she said and laughed. Her voice was so good. She was so cute. Her hair, her body, her nose especially,

Vikram laughed, and they talked with each other for a long time, a really long time.

"Sabhi yaatri kripya dhyaan de, Ahmedabad jaane wale viman taiyaar hain, kuch hi der mein hum Ahmedabad ke liye rawana ho jayenge, dhanyavad!" (All passengers please note. The flight to Ahmedabad will be boarding soon, thank you!)" said a speaker. Her voice was not as good as the previous one.

"Ok dear, we are leaving, so take care, bye bye!" said Vikram and cut the call. He felt relieved for some time because of Maisha but now he was tense again for a reason when he remembered something he had forgotten.

Suddenly his eyes fell on a beggar outside the airport, when he was roaming for something. She was not begging at that time but she was carrying her child. They were dirty, nobody gave a care about them. Vikram felt odd at that time. Surely it is common in India, but why? Everything *bad* is common in India. This is hell!

He felt worried about ViraT. He hoped for the best. He went to the plane, and they left the airport.

❧

They are humans, surely as we are for the sake

They are in misery and we are in a fake,

They wander here and there, for what we already have.

Why are we being selfish for what God gave?

Surely, they seem small to most of us.

They cry for food while we sit on a bus,

Why do they cry and wander; are they mad?

Are they out of their mind, or just being sad?

We don't care, do we? Just for ourselves, we do what we want.

We just care for each other and hunt them with a taunt,

They are weak, and we are mighty, just like Superman.

We throw tons of food, and they look for it in a dustbin,

They put their hands forward even though they should not

They just lie on streets as we do on a cot,

They want alms, and we want millions for nothing.

There is no such song that we sing that they don't sing,

They breathe, they eat, they drink, but less than us.

They want some money and we waste that on fuss.

Can't we do anything for God's sake to bring equality in between?

They need love and care, but why are we not keen?

He was on the plane, keen to look outside. He thought of nothing but his future. Would he succeed in changing India or would he fail? If he wins, then he will become an example for the people. If he loses, then someone else must come to complete the work. He was curious about how he would succeed. He had not even been on the wanted list. He somehow wanted to be on the list. He wanted people to know him. After people know him, he will then start the real work. Finally, they landed in Ahmedabad. He was worried and tense.

"Driver *bhai*, take me to the main chowk here and stop at house no. 15," Vikram told the driver when he made him stop.

"Yes, sir, come!" told the driver enthusiastically.

Vikram was again thinking if he would lose the battle. He was irritated when this thought came to him repeatedly. He wanted to get rid of this thought. They were moving at a decent speed. He was looking outside from the window.

It was shocking! A blast happened in a big building. It was very large. It was shining in the beautiful blue sky and radiations from the sun. The blast shook the city. The cars stopped. Some even crashed.

"What the hell!" shouted Vikram, and the driver was silent and awestruck.

Vikram stepped out of the car as many of them did. The building was down, killing hundreds and thousands of people.

"HELL!" said Vikram and moved towards the building, barefoot. But there it was, the police. It stopped him and everyone, and many people were crying and moaning. It was something that is not common. It must be a terrorist attack. But why in Ahmedabad?

Vikram tried to call Virat, but he was unreachable. Vikram visited his home.

Vikram knocked on the door several times.

"Hello!" said Vikram to a lady when she opened the door.

"Namaste!" she replied and invited him inside.

The house was old-fashioned, made up of bricks and mud. The condition looked poor. It was shocking.

Vikram settled down and drank the glass of water, which she offered him.

"Where is Virat?" asked Vikram immediately after drinking the water.

"Will you want some tea?" asked the girl, pretending she did not hear something.

"No! I mean no, I just want to know where is Virat?" he said stiffly at first but then he changed his tone.

She cried! She was in tears. What was the reason? It seemed like hell. Vikram was amazed and shocked. Why would she cry when he told her about Virat?

"We don't have any mo-money!" she said and cried again.

"What money?" asked Vikram, surprised.

"Everyone comes for borrowed money. He is dead, I don't have any. Please don't ask for more money. I have sold all my gold!" she said while crying and hiccupping.

"Listen, sister, I am not here for any money," said Vikram, and now she was shocked and surprised.

"Then?" she asked him, still amazed, and hiccupped.

"I just want to know where he is. He did not talk to me for a while," said Vikram.

"Well, thank you for coming here. He may be dead, and my whole family may be dead. I couldn't find them anywhere.

The whole society is blaming him; since then, he has never been found…" she said and started weeping.

"Well, sorry, but how were you related to him?" asked Vikram to the woman. She seemed to be confident now.

"I am his wife," she said quickly and firmly. It seemed that she didn't care what she belonged to him.

"Oh! I am sorry!" said Vikram just for formality, and he didn't feel sorry.

"Don't be sorry, what do you do and why do you look for him?" asked the woman.

"Well, I-I am his friend from UP," he bluffed, and maybe the woman did not trust him fully.

He left the house and reached the building. It was destroyed. The police were there. There was a dead body. It had been tortured. A van left it here. It didn't seem to be dead because of the blast. And to his surprise, it was no one but…

"Virat!" he said and bent down to check him.

"Sir, please move from there. Don't touch anything or you will be in danger."

Vikram nodded and then looked at Virat. He seemed to be badly tortured. He had been killed by many people. He was not wearing a shirt. His belly was cut open, and his renal artery was exposed.

They took every dead body for a forensic report, for postmortem, and all the evidence. A task force was set out to investigate the case.

It seemed out of mind for Vikram. It was just hell. Vikram couldn't come up with anything.

After some time, he went to the police for more information. At first, they didn't allow, but after Vikram pleaded very hard and gave them something, they allowed him.

He saw the body, and a man was with it.

"Hi," said Vikram to the man and sat down on another chair beside the man.

"Hi, well, do you want to know about this person?" asked the man. He had already gotten information from the police.

"Yes, sir, I want to know everything about this man," said Vikram and waited for the response.

"Well, this body was particularly murdered by the group that attacked the building, I strongly believe," said the man, who was looking into documents.

"Why?" asked Vikram curiously.

"Maybe some personal conflict," said the man.

"What have they done?" asked Vikram while looking at the dead body.

"They have brutally killed him. They have taken the kidneys, lungs, testes, and some bones," said the man and again concentrated on his papers.

"Why will they do so?" asked Vikram, who was shocked by the statement.

"How will I know? It needs investigation," replied the man. He told Vikram to leave, and he did so. He left the station.

❧

He booked his flight to Varanasi. He reached there. He met everyone. Karan was also there. They relaxed a bit. Vikram told them everything. They were also shocked.

Karan had made Vikram a friend again. Vikram also didn't mind. But the main thing that made him go crazy was the death of Virat. Who will do that and why? It seemed just madness.

He wanted to know everything about Virat. He also wanted to know everything about the attack on the buildings because the man said that the attacker group killed Virat. He was ready to face another challenge.

❧

Vikram contacted everyone to reach his house. The people were Majid, Maisha, and Karan. They were his closest ones, except Karan. No one else cared much. He wanted to solve the case himself. In midway, he also wanted to get more states under control. That work was given to Majid. So, he had no contribution to solving the case but full contribution to rising and making The Legend's Club. He was ready and accepted it. He went on his journey.

Now remained the three. They needed to solve it. Maisha was not given much responsibility, but the main members were Vikram and Karan. They wanted to solve the case.

❧

Now something unexpected happened. A man knocked on the door and then came inside the room when Vikram allowed him. He saw Vikram and gazed at him until he sat down on a chair. He cried and hugged him. At first, Vikram tried to get rid of him, but when he hugged, kissed, and cried for him, he felt something strange. Vikram eased the man. He seemed somewhat familiar.

"Who are you?" asked Vikram elegantly.

"Dear, I am Vijay!"

Life is hell confusing; actually, life is a challenge. It is full of plot twists. It is just plain wrong. Life brings everything with it, whether it is joy, sadness, or anger. This time, it was everything. Life takes you anywhere. Anything can happen at any time. It is hellishly confusing.

They talked to each other. Vikram didn't believe it was Vijay, his elder brother.

"But how are you alive?" asked Vikram while he couldn't control his tears. His heart said that it was Vijay and he was sure, but he wanted to ask.

"Did you see me die?" asked Vijay.

"No, but..."

"Well, when you went for water, I went for water too. I knew that the bathroom water would be bad, so I went to look outside. When I looked outside, thousands of men were running towards the temple and I knew whom it would be. Abdul Majid, son of a bitch!" said Vijay and wept his tears.

"What the hell!" shouted Majid who was there at that time.

"Who are you?" asked Vijay.

"I AM Abdul Majid!" said Majid and surprised everyone except Vikram.

"What the hell!" shouted Karan and Vijay in unison. They didn't know that this man could be Abdul Majid, the man who killed many innocent people.

Vijay almost jumped on him.

"STOP!" shouted Vikram and everyone was numb. "Stop! We will look after this after some time, first tell me what happened?"

"But this man…"

"Stop, tell me what happened?" asked Vikram and didn't let him do anything.

"Just tell me what he is doing with you if he was - why?" asked Vijay, who got a bit emotional.

"I will tell you, but first tell me what happened in the temple," said Vikram.

"Well, when I saw them, I was numb. Anything I could do was to run inside the temple. I went inside and hid in a cabinet in a room where they keep the tools," said Vijay and took a short pause and sighed, "I hid in that and heard many cries and shouts. I was crying. After some time, someone entered the room to look for anyone. I suddenly made a noise and thought I was done, but luckily he went out."

"FUCK!" shouted Vikram in regret and tears.

"What happened?" asked Karan empathetically.

"It was me!" he said and took his brother's hand in his. "I went inside and heard a voice or sound, but I didn't care about it and left!"

"Shit!" said Vijay, and they hugged each other.

"But how did you know about me here?" asked Vikram in a shock.

"I thought you were gone. I lived alone and continued to get an MBA after much struggle. Leave it. When I came to Banaras and heard about an influencer, Vikram Rathore, I believed that it might be someone else, maybe a politician. But then I came to know about your goal and all that. I saw you. I was shocked. I wanted to reach you but there was no way. Security wouldn't allow me. Finally, I made a formal but illegal appointment to come to the house here!" he said, and Vikram smiled and cried at the same time.

He was happy. They talked about each other. They joked and talked. Vikram acted like he truly believed the man. How could the man be Vijay and still be alive? How did he know about me? But the one thing that made him think was how did he know about the bathroom, water, and the thud in the cabinet.

"But what about this Majid?" asked Vijay.

"Well, this is a long story!"

"Just tell me nah!"

Vikram narrated the whole story until he left Majid's family. He told them everything up to that point.

"After I left the house, I was alone. If I wanted to do anything, I wanted to kill this man. I was alone. I had no money. And the biggest problem was that I didn't even know where he was!"

PART 5

SEVERAL YEARS AGO

13

A Foe To Friend

Vikram was alone. He didn't know what to do or how to find Majid to kill. He had a fire in his heart. He just wanted his death and by his own hands. He was penniless and landless and friendless and powerless.

He wanted some help. He decided to ask locals.

"Hello, uncle," said Vikram to a shopkeeper who was chewing paan at that time.

"Hi," said the man in a fat voice because of the paan.

"Uncle, I wanted to know where the police take the criminals,"

"Where are you from?"

"Here only,"

"Well, do you have brains?"

"Why?"

"Obviously they will take them to jail,"

"I know, but which jail?"

"Depends,"

"Well, what about big criminals?"

"Like?"

"Abdul Majid,"

"Listen, kid. You get outta here or you will be wiped like a snake from the path, is that clear?"

"Well, I just want to know where they keep him,"

"Are you his relative?"

"No,"

"Then what is the problem?"

"I want to kill him,"

❧

He was thrown out of all places. He was not answered. He was confused. He remembered and regretted because he could have told Majid's family where the oldest man of the family lives. Tihar or wherever.

❧

He went back to the family. He reached the house. He had been out of the house for weeks. He rang the bell, and Arshid Ahmad's wife came out.

"Vikram!" she said in surprise, "Where were you?"

"Can you tell me where your father-in-law is?" asked Vikram coldly without even caring for the lady.

"Come in first..."

"No, just tell me, where is your father-in-law?" asked Vikram.

She sighed and said, "In jail."

"Well, I know, but which jail?" asked Vikram impatiently.

"Tihar..."

Vikram just ran away swiftly. She shouted and cried for him, but he didn't care. She even ran and fell down, but he didn't even look back. He was stone-hearted. He ran away. He thought that he had seen one boy also with her later when she ran.

Now the biggest problem was how he would go to Delhi?

He knew if he got money everything is possible. But now, the biggest problem was from where to get the money. He decided to steal money. That would get him money. He didn't care whether it was right or wrong. He wanted money.

He went to a shopkeeper. He had some money with him, enough to last him a few days.

"Uncle, can you give me an ice cream?"

"Yes, why not?" he said and went behind to get ice cream. It was a pretty decent-sized store. Vikram was already inside. When the man went to the backside near the fridges, Vikram tried to open a drawer. There it was! Money! Lots! He just took it and put it in his pocket. The man came and gave him ice cream. Vikram threw the note down. The man sighed and bent to take the note. When he was finally up, he couldn't find the little boy again. He was amazed and found it absurd. He was surprised. But when he opened the drawer, he was more surprised.

⤝

Vikram had stolen much money. He had bought himself many bags and clothes. He bought new things. He had a backpack. He had a small bag attached to his belly like a belt. He had much money. But then he didn't find it enough.

He was eighteen already. He had done many small robberies. He had forgotten every dream, every loved one. He just wanted money. After money, he wanted Abdul Majid.

He decided to loot just one more time, but this time, it was going to be a huge heist.

He decided to rob a bank. He first wanted to know about the bank. It was not a big bank. Not a national or international level bank. Obviously, he was not going to rob SBI or RBI for God's sake. It was a famous local bank. It was huge. It had many branches, and one branch was in Lucknow. He went to Lucknow. After a year, the heist was done. It took him everything. Many were dead because of him. Some farmers had committed suicide because of him. It was the great Indian Heist!

After the heist was done, after selling all the precious things like diamonds, he acquired a wealth of about more than 800 crores. He decided to go to Delhi. He knew that the man was in Tihar.

He booked the flight to Delhi. He was in business class. He was planning how to get Abdul out of jail. He wanted to kill him alone. Not just kill, but torture. It was a thing of satisfaction for him.

He reached Delhi and stayed at a hotel at night. He planned to get himself out of the jail. He had come up with an idea.

Next day, he reached the court. He wanted a trial for Majid. After all the formalities, the court accepted. He had some people ready.

"Where is the accused?" asked the judge impatiently.

"He may be coming, your honour; he is with the police," replied Vikram.

But to the surprise of all, he didn't reach. They got news that the police van was attacked on the way and Majid was released. They said that the attackers were some old criminals who wanted to kill a police officer in the van because he had once done wrong to them, in their opinion. The news was sent by some police officers. The court was dismissed. Some people thought Vikram may be the culprit, but he explained himself and saved himself.

Majid was taken to an old shed. Vikram reached there. There were some gangsters around him. They were hired by Vikram. Majid's mouth was covered with a scarf. Vikram removed the scarf, and Majid started panting.

"Well, Majid, do you remember me?" asked Vikram coldly.

"WH-what…" he said breathlessly.

"I am Vikram Rathore, son of Rathore Singh!"

Majid finally felt relieved.

"WHAT?" he said firmly, in surprise.

"You thought that I would forget, well you thought I am dead anyway,"

"See Vikram, there is a huge misunderstanding…"

"Don't tell me anything, you old bastard!"

"What will you do?"

"I will kill you!" he replied firmly.

"Ok kill me!"

"What? What do you mean?"

"Kill me! But before that, I want to tell you something,"

"What?"

"The reason I broke into the house is not because I hated you because you were of a different religion,"

"What! Then?"

"Your grandfather, Balbir Singh, was not an innocent old man. He had killed thousands of people in the riots decades ago. Well, your father, Rathore, was not innocent either. He was something you can never imagine. I believe that I shall get the punishment for what I have done. But believe me, it was not me who killed the people in the temple. It was Kiran Mehta Singh. He wanted to kill them. He knew that no one would support him, so he killed them. Whether they were innocent or not, he killed them. I was hiding at that time. Your grandmother was shocked by all that. I took her to the hospital, but because of all the chaos, she died of a heart attack. I surrendered because I knew that I was wrong. I just wanted to kill the criminals of the past, but I forgot that that work would be done by Allah Himself."

"But…"

"Shoot me, Vikram. I wanted to create India a better place. But because of your grandfather, I had to enter the game of blood to stop him. But it led to some other consequences."

Vikram was shocked. The man wanted to change India.

"Your son, I lived with them, but when I heard that you…"

"My son?"

"Arshid Ahmad,"

"He is not my son. He is…"

"He is what?"

"I bought him from an orphanage."

"He is dead anyway!"

"WHAT!"

"Yes, he was killed by some gang years ago!"

Majid started to weep. He was shocked. He was fed up. He wanted to die really.

"Kill me, my son!"

Vikram felt something. He didn't want to kill him. He wanted to let him live. He wanted to live with him. At that time, he felt that he was the worst person on earth. He left a family in the worst time. He looted a bank for some money. He brought the old man just to find out that his family were killers.

"Old man, come on, let's live life to the fullest!"

PART 6
SEVERAL YEARS LATER

14

In The Valley

Many states were under his influence. Vikram had made his mark almost everywhere. He was not stopping until the government noticed everything. There was an arrest warrant out for him. He was not considered a big criminal until he killed many criminals. He was a saviour for the people. They praised him. However, the majority of places remained unvisited. Majid could have done that, but the police were everywhere looking for them. Vikram had delivered powerful speeches and even lured the toughest individuals. But now he was facing one of his toughest enemies, the Central Government.

"The Supreme Court of India has issued an arrest warrant against Vikram Rathore," said a reporter.

Vikram had become a wanted criminal. He was considered harmful. Police looked for him.

Vikram didn't care about anything. He wanted to see who killed Virat and attacked the mall. It was his main motto at that time.

"Vikram, I found out that the killer lies in Himachal Pradesh. They were sent by some person to kill you. They wanted you to get a hint of danger. This time they may attack you," said Karan while they were in a house.

They had taken refuge in an old house because the police were finding them.

"Then we shall move to Himachal Pradesh,"

"But won't someone catch us, especially the police," said Abdul Majid.

"I think we shall find out any trick to go and find the killers and the one who owns them,"

"What trick?"

"Well, I guess that no one knows you in Himachal Pradesh, so you should visit as someone from the government," suggested Abdul Majid.

"But I think that won't help," said Karan uncomfortably.

"I think as an IAS officer no one will catch me," said Vikram.

"But what about security and proofs?" asked Majid, and Karan nodded.

"Well, what does he even do?" said Vikram while pointing to Karan.

Vikram, after he narrated the story of his meeting with Majid, met Majid. They were alone. They found a room. Majid was feeling sad and uncomfortable because Vikram had lied about their meeting. The case was not the same.

"Why did you lie?" asked Majid.

"I had to," he replied. "If I think, then I will reveal the truth…"

Suddenly, Maisha opened the door of the room.

"What are you people doing here?" she asked, oddly.

"Just talking…"

"Vikram?"

"Yes?"

"Why did you not explain the heist you had done?"

"Well, I will, some time else!"

Everything will not be hidden, but will be revealed!

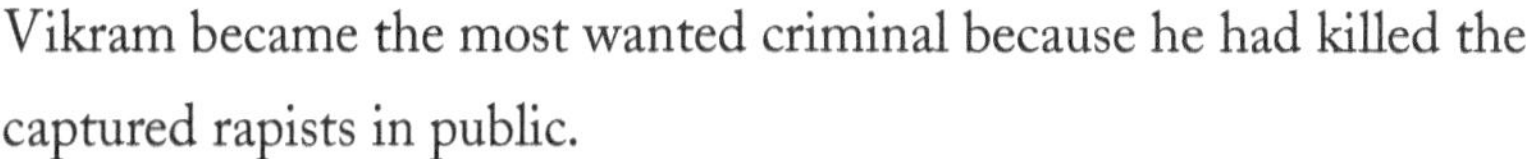

Vikram became the most wanted criminal because he had killed the captured rapists in public.

"Well, Vikram Rathore, the person who wants to create his own government in India, has done something that flouts the law. He thinks that he is the messiah of the people. He recently did something horrible. He posted it on social media. Rarely! He showed the rapists he had captured. This incident occurred on the Ludhiana side of Punjab. He killed them using an AK-47 in front of the public. The police want him, and the notice has been sent by the prime minister himself."

"These reporters are just going the other way," said Majid as he was with Vikram in Punjab.

"I think I shall get a haircut,"

"What the hell are you talking about?"

"I want my hair and beard different for Himachal Pradesh,"

"Police will catch you! They are outside looking for you!"

"I am going…"

Majid tried his best to stop him but didn't succeed. Finally, Majid gave up and prayed to God for his safety.

Vikram reached outside the barber shop. The barber seemed too modern *chapri*. The shop was on the road. The door was open. He could see the green fields of Punjab from there. The shop was quite small, but the air coming was fresh. There was not much hustle and bustle of cars on that road.

"Hello, sir, sit down until I get ready!" said the barber. He seemed not to know Vikram.

"Ok," he replied casually.

Vikram was sitting and looking outside at green farms. He was at that time in a village. The land was vast. It was the best scene he had seen. Such beautiful crops. Suddenly, police cars were moving outside. They seemed to be in a rush. Vikram smiled. He knew that they would find him somewhere in a secret place while he was setting up his beard in a public shop.

He was done. He reached the house. Majid told him everything about how he should not go out and all that. He ignored him and left for Himachal Pradesh alone in a car. Police were around him. They were giving him security. They were not real policemen. They were hired by Karan for Vikram.

He had an official IAS rank. That surely was made by illegal techniques. He used his name *Varun Mehta*, his friend from old school. He also wanted to become an IAS officer, but he couldn't because of the massacre, and he died. He wanted to revive his feelings in himself.

After a very, very long drive, he reached Shimla. There, he met his rental car waiting for him.

Karan had kidnapped the real IAS officer and set Vikram in place of him. He had his appearance different from usual. Nobody could notice him much. He had taken his name and all his belongings.

There he saw his assistant, Manoj, and driver, and a man who was sitting on the front seat casually.

They picked him, greeted him, and did all they could, but Vikram remained silent mostly.

He went to a location given by Karan. There was nothing: an old house. He decided to go inside. He went inside and opened each and every door, but he could see nothing. He went to the upper floor and found nothing there. The house seemed Anglo-Indian in style. When he got out of the house, something terrible happened. He was alone in the area. He thought he would find the man there because Karan had given him the address.

Several masked men came in front of him with long swords. They looked terrifying. Again, swords!

"Vikram Rathore, the man who created his own government of India!" said a man with a very masculine tone. "See, mister Vikram, I am gonna kill you right now!"

"Why?" asked Vikram coolly.

"I wanted you!" he replied uncomfortably.

Suddenly, police forces came from surrounding areas. They were Vikram's people. They had guns.

"Drop your weapons, people!" said Vikram coolly again.

"Who are they?" asked the man after seeing the silencers at the end of their guns.

"Your death!" said Vikram and moved his finger in the air.

After a few seconds, they all lay down on the ground without any soul. His men took them to secret places to bury them. They were done. Vikram had kept the forces around him for safety because he knew that he could get attacked.

"You were right, Karan, they were there!" said Vikram while he was in his hotel room.

"Did they attack you?" asked Karan quickly.

"Yes, but I attacked them before they could move," replied Vikram and laughed. Karan also made a fake laugh from the other side.

He decided to leave.

"Why?" asked Majid on the phone.

"I don't want to know more. I can find more people, and I don't care!"

"Your choice!" replied Majid and cut the call. Vikram had his own mobile with him.

"Manoj," said Vikram stiffly.

"Yes, sir!" said the assistant quickly.

"I have some work, move to *Delhi*!"

The car was moving at a decent speed along the beautiful hillsides of Himachal Pradesh!

15

The Rise of Legend

Majid was shocked when he heard that Vikram was dead. Maisha became unconscious. Majid was crying. He even tried to jerk her and wake her up again, but she was badly injured.

"What the hell do you mean he is dead?" he shouted stiffly.

"Sir, I can understand, but doctors said so!" he replied and left.

Majid was unstable. He called Karan, but the call was not reachable.

"Why the hell do these people not come up when you need them?" he said to himself and cried more and more.

He admitted Maisha first and then went to the doctors. A lady doctor was there.

"Madam, have you seen Vik - sorry, Varun Mehta?" he asked her.

"Yes, sir, he has been taken outside for some purposes,"

"What purposes?" he asked.

"I don't know, you shall go and find out."

⋐

Manoj came to the old man, who was sitting alone on a bench with a gloom of the greatest.

"Hey, sir?" he said to Majid.

"Yes," he replied with a broken voice.

"Can I ask you something?" he asked, expecting a yes.

"Of course," replied Majid, and he became hopeful.

"Can you tell me, how did Vikram become the greatest criminal in the history of India?"

"Do you really want to know?" he asked to ensure.

"Yes,"

When Vikram decided that Majid would go to other states, he wanted to stay back at first. After some time, he would move and influence everyone.

He wanted to know who killed Virat first. He wanted to know about the killer.

Majid was already in many states. He had given people some hint of a man coming to change the country and its fate. He had told people that a man will come, who will end the poverty and crisis. He will create his own government.

Vikram started to investigate the Gujarat attacks. They seemed suspicious. No one could guess who attacked. Some people guessed that some terrorist group might do it. But Vikram knew that this was not done by any such group. Why would a terrorist group kill Virat personally?

"Maybe he might have known about their plans and decided to stop them, but they killed him," said Maisha. Well, she was also right. It was a theory but was practical enough.

"No!" replied Vikram confidently.

"How do you know?" asked Maisha while Karan was silently listening to them.

"Because I have seen and felt Virat. He won't stop them without consulting me. I know he won't give his life for nothing," replied Vikram.

"Well, that is also right. I guess let me do the investigation and you go to people for work," suggested Karan with a very quick voice.

"I trust you, so I let you do the work," said Vikram and Karan nodded.

Maisha was surprised that Karan showed up suddenly to help; however, she remained silent.

Vikram decided to leave for Tamil Nadu first.

He reached Tamil Nadu. He organised a big campaign there. He invited all people. He even offered free refreshments.

Well, the campaign could hold lakhs of people. Around 2 lakh. It was a huge gathering, the biggest in history. People gathered. They were interested because they were told that a man would help them but wouldn't even touch politics.

Everything was dependent on his speech. He gave a dashing speech. It attracted many people. He told them to cooperate with him and his team. He wanted them to support The Legend's Club. He told them that he wanted to overthrow the government and create his own. He would create a big economy. The constitution and everything will be the same but the rulers won't be. He told them that he would rule with them. He told them that he would end poverty.

"Greetings everyone! I am Vikram Rathore, even though my friend tells me that I have no family, but I replied that I have *you!*" he said while pointing to the people. They cheered. "I am here for no cause of elections or votes, but I am here for the cause of the greatest. I have been attacked, almost killed just because I wanted my society to prosper. Sometimes, I was deviated from the path, but just because of you people, I was back to normal but with more hopes and more ambitions for your success. I know what the government wants. I am not going against the government, but I am challenging them.

"I will provide you with everything, but I need you to follow me as your leader. I want every bad trait from my society vanished. If you wonder what I mean by society, that is my country and you people!" he continued, and there was a huge applause. "We want betterment of our country, of our state, but by supporting the people who are not aware of anything but just money and power, then it is not possible. Support me and see how I reform the country. I won't work with my own will but will strictly follow the guidelines of the constitution. I know that making a government is also a part of the constitution but not a government which is greedy, corrupted, and manipulative. You know, when I feel that our country has formed the best government, I promise that I will step down on my own.

Elections will happen, but until the good party won't lead, I will lead. I want my people to be safe and happy.

"I will provide you all the necessities like water, electricity, and transport, etc. I wonder if it is just our country that yearns for things like roads. It should have been completed by the government a long time ago. Leave it; I will do whatever you want. Just trust me. Any questions?"

"How can we trust you? You might be doing it for your benefit," questioned a man from the audience.

"You don't want to trust me, right? Don't trust me. Trust the government that loots you. Well, they loot you and you don't even get a hint. Banks are looting you and the government is mixed. You want your loans to stay stuck forever, right? Don't trust me. Everything great does not get support. Everything is because of you people. You won't support the good but will support the looters!"

The people applauded loudly. They cried for him. They cried his name, "Vikram Rathore!" very hard.

The main thing about Guts was that he was live on social media. Everyone was watching him, and of course, the government. Vikram didn't fear. He wanted a fair rule and *his* rule.

Due to his motivation, people started to beat corrupt officers. Even ministers were killed. The army was failing. Not in one state. But in many states. He had done the magic. Farmers were on the road. Everyone was demanding the government to surrender.

This was the first time in the history of India that people forced the government to surrender and give up powers.

Shops were closed. No man was at work. The economy was shut down. People just wanted the rule of The Legend's Club.

Meanwhile, Vikram was uploading video after video. He was targeting the government and wanted his rule. He wanted India to be in a revolution. A revolution where everyone is equal, where there is no corruption, discrimination, or breaking of laws.

People were going mad. They were forcing the prime minister himself to surrender and give Vikram the seat. Even though Vikram told people that he didn't want politics, still people wanted him to become the prime minister.

After that, the government and the prime minister himself started to find and kill him.

They demanded the dead body of Vikram. They were not answered. They were told that the body is at the postmortem in forensic. They just wanted to see him. They were not allowed.

Suddenly the driver, who was alarmed, came to their room with a serious and grave face.

"What! Mahesh, you are here? You were admitted, right?" asked Manoj with a surprised face.

"Well, I have to be!" he replied gravely and coldly.

"Why?" asked Majid. "And who allowed you? Were you not hospitalised for a serious injury?"

"Well, yes, but when the truth is hidden, we have to bring it to others!" he replied and shocked Majid as he remembered that these were the exact same words of Vikram.

"You know Vikram?" asked Majid seriously.

"Wait, how can he know, he was not here…"

"It is not important whether I was here or not," interrupted Mahesh, "Well, I knew him a long time ago."

"When?" asked Manoj.

"Well, do you remember when I told you to let me keep the identity and photo of the new IAS officer hidden so that it would be a surprise for you?"

"Yes, so?" replied Manoj.

"Well, I was already in his team. I knew his ambitions and I recognised him. I decided to work for him and help him and promised him to keep it a secret, but now it is an emergency."

"Well! But what were you talking about and what are you doing here?" asked Manoj while Majid saw their hanging faces.

"Well, I wasn't unconscious fully; I was just sleeping and these illiterate doctors today! Vikram is not dead!" he said and shocked everyone.

"What do you mean? Doctors said, right?" said Majid with a hopeful face.

"Well, the prime minister's people themselves came here in disguise. They paid the hospital well and took Vikram with them and took him somewhere!"

"Fuck!" shouted Majid, stiffly, and it made him cough.

"What should we do now?" asked Manoj.

"We have to get Vikram back," said Majid, "or else they will kill him!"

"Why will they kill him?" demanded Manoj.

"Because he was with truth!" replied Mahesh. Well, he didn't seem to be so philosophical and mysterious, but he was. He seemed like an average driver, but he was on the next level.

"How will we get him back?" asked Manoj. Everyone thought.

"Well, we won't get him back!" said Majid and shocked the others again.

"Then?" asked Manoj.

"They will give him back!"

"How?" asked Manoj and Mahesh in unison.

"First get Maisha and tell her that the guy is alive!"

16

The Killer and the End

Maisha got to know everything, and she seemed relaxed. Well, she was obsessed with Vikram badly. She wanted him badly. He was loved by anyone he would talk to. And the same was the case with Maisha and others.

Majid told them his plan. They were relaxed after hearing the plan. But the problem was, will they succeed in their plan?

"We need the help of Karan here," said Majid and dialled his number.

"Hello?" asked Majid.

"Hello," said Karan nonchalantly.

"Well, I have good news and I will need your help," said Majid.

"What?" he said in alarm.

"Well, we found Vikram. He is alive!" said Majid happily.

Karan didn't reply for a few seconds.

"That is really good news, my friend, but how do you know?" he said with an awkward voice.

"Well, he is with the PM himself and we have to get him!"

"How?" asked Karan excitedly.

Majid narrated his whole plan. It seemed good for Karan. He approved and decided to help. After all, Vikram was alive.

Majid arranged many cars and police officers with the help of Karan. Majid's plan was something extraordinary. He wanted to kidnap the PM himself. The biggest kidnapping in history. Well, they were forming history. The kidnapping was not as illogical as it seemed but was fully planned. They would get Vikram easily if the plan was successful. It was planned well and all the things were ready. It was going to take a huge effort. Even timings were done. Every second was allotted to a man. In the end, they would get the PM and they would be good.

They were on a national highway. The city was visible as they were moving through it. They were in trucks, huge ones. Maybe around fifteen trucks. It had all the needed things. But something struck them.

All the electric billboards and all the TVs showed Vikram! Well, opposite of Majid's thoughts. He thought that if such a thing happens, Vikram will be under PM and he will get the punishment. But he was wrong! Life takes turns and that is when life gets good and exciting. When there are no plot twists, there are no great endings.

The video was live. It was a dark room. Vikram was full of blood. He was standing and PM himself was kneeling. Vikram was pointing a gun at the head of the PM. A speaker was attached to Vikram. He was looking towards the camera with a bloody face.

"To all the people, let me tell you today. I am Vikram Rathore. I have hacked the internet of India. Not because I am a hacker but because I hack."

"Well, let me tell you today. If I have any identity, let me tell you today. I have the PM today because he didn't have us before. He has been a minister for more than three decades if not a PM for three decades. Where was he and his party when something happened? And that incident is the reason I am here and he is under my hand. My hand decides his life."

"Well, I am one of the two survivors of the great Indian Massacre. Yes, that is true. I was a kid. If you find a note on the wall of the stairs, it was written by me on that bloody day. I survived because fate wanted me to. And fate wanted it because I would be here and I am. Well, my brother also survived the massacre. But leave all this. Does that define my identity, I always think. But now I can answer myself, no! That is not the reason for my identity; that was just fate.

"But my identity should be what my fate wanted me to do. If we are not ahead today, we are the reason. Let me start from the beginning. And you *PM*, stay here and don't talk. I will come to the point why this man is here. All the securities would be finding me now but believe me they can't. Leave it. Why are we lacking? Why aren't we prospering? Why are always there bad things happening all around our country? Well, the answer is we. We don't want it to prosper. What do we think? We think why Muslims are ahead, why Hindus are ahead, why Sikhs are ahead, and why Christians are ahead. We think why he is better than me. Why will they be better than us? They are impure. They are inferiors. India is ahead in discrimination and all types of these social diseases. Why? Why are we letting down the thoughts of our freedom fighters? Our fighters wanted the country free so that we live like humans. But no! We just urge each other to fight for religious reasons. We are just here to degrade each other."

"Everyone thinks how he could earn better but no one thinks how our country can earn better. Earning does not mean money, but the nationalism and the patriotism. Why should our country be better, right? Some support other countries even though they have given you nothing. In cricket and games, that is fine but in terms of other domains, no! No means No! It is our country, our competition for development is not with our own people but with other countries. There are some insects in our society who defame each other on the basis of religion, caste, creed, and profession.

"Why? Why aren't we living in fraternity? Ask our politicians; they will say that they can give life for the soul of the constitution. Then why are they promoting hate? We are brothers and sisters. We are humans first. Youth believes in what others tell them. Even my grandfather, who was a terrorist, urged me to hate Muslims and Hindus. I couldn't figure out that he was wrong, but for some goodness, I never believed him. Because I was naughty and clever. What hurts me most is that my own father was. But I don't want you to be like that. You are my family. That means if all the people of India are my family, then all the people of India are each other's family. The best thing about thinking, understanding, and what I later understood, the spirit of the constitution is that I live with my best friend. My best friend, who was my greatest enemy. Well, my best friend is right now innocent, but once he was most wanted by the government and as well as for me. He killed my family. And now I understand that it was fate and it was for good.

"You don't have to give up. Not because your own people poison you. Well, if we learn to forgive, we become the greatest. Every religion is interrelated, if we dive deep in. But today's orthodox blind-faithed people, they spread hate. Why don't we make them understand that we are fighting for nothing? People kill each other for nothing. They seem to be demons to them, but they are also humans. We are brothers. It is our country, our responsibility. We have to take care. History is witness that when everyone is united, nothing can stop Indians. I know it seems odd to speak, but we have to make it practical. We have to protect the soul of our constitution. Other countries are well having fun while we are making fun of our own country. They are developed because they know that they have to equally contribute. There are no communal riots. There is no Hindu-Muslim divide. We have to unite. Well, talking about this man. This is just shit! Hey, tell them the truth!"

"What truth? I don't know what you are talking about!" stuttered the PM. This was the first time in history when people saw a thing that terrorised even the cruellest of the terrorisers.

The public as well as the government were shocked. What the hell was happening? Maisha was happy to see Vikram alive. She began to sob. Abdul Majid knew that there was some problem. Army trucks were moving in quantities of hundreds through each road.

"Well, man, tell me, or you see the gun?" warned Vikram again and was ready with the pistol.

"I don't know…"

SHOT! The prime minister found or just *seen* dead. No censorship, *no bakwas just seedhi baat*! Everyone was shocked. There was the greatest instability in India ever.

"Don't panic, let me tell you why I killed the man," said Vikram with a cool voice. Manoj was surprised to see the same face and manner he had seen in the restaurant.

"Well, the reason that he is dead today is great. He was not a deserving one. He is a liar. He is playing with your emotions. He creates societies on the basis of religion. Before we end criminals we shall end the ig ones who are actually responsible. The recent army officers, who were found dead while fighting with a terrorist group, their killings are upon him. He killed them. He was not a good leader, to be sincere. And I am! Well, I don't or I am not overconfident but I feel. I know that India and the whole world can be changed. Today, the reason I am here was already written in fate. And when something happens, it happens for the good!"

Suddenly, all the screens were normal, and the ad of Godrej products was shown on the billboard where Abdul Majid was.

Majid was alone sitting at home when the bell rang. He went to open the door and was shocked to see Vikram along with Maisha.

"Vikram! What? Where?…"

"Relax, old man. Just sit down and relax. Talk slowly or your arteries will blast in a second," said Vikram humorously and made Maisha smile.

They were all inside.

❦

"I lied about the PM!" said Vikram.

"Then?" asked Majid.

"I will tell you, but can you do me a favour?"

"What?"

"Well, can you call Karan?" asked Vikram.

"Why?"

"Well, I want to talk to him because I have some work, but don't tell him I am here,"

"OK!"

Majid called Karan. He first declined but after insisting a lot, he had to concede. Majid told him something that he had to come.

After some time, the bell rang again. Majid went and opened the door.

"Hey Majid! How are you, my friend?" he asked very vibrantly.

"I am good, come in!" replied Majid, and they both went inside.

He was walking and smiling until he saw Vikram, polishing his 'pistol with a silencer'.

"Vi- Vikram!" he said and was shocked to his deepest roots.

"Hi, dear politician, sit down!" replied Vikram and made him sit.

But to everyone's surprise except Vikram's, Karan fell at Vikram's knees and cried.

"Sorry Vikram! I am really sorry. Forgive me!" he begged, and everyone was shocked.

SHOT! Again, a man was lying dead on the tiles. Bloody Vikram was feeling most comfortable.

"WHAT THE FUCK!" shouted Maisha. She was crying.

"Don't worry, dear, again!" Vikram replied coolly.

"What?" said Maisha with a scared-to-hell face.

"Imposter detected!" he replied. "Can I explain and end the story at once?"

"Tell me, Vikram, what has happened to you?" said Majid with his most tense voice.

"Well, let me begin again. You know the day I told you he would invite me back to his party?"

"Yes, so?"

"Well, I told you he gave me some money and that is why. But that is not the reason! The reason is something else. Something that might even shock you. In return, he wanted to kill me and I knew this from the beginning."

"Well, he lied to me and told me to go to Himachal Pradesh where the killers are. He had even planned an attack on me and I had already prepared forces. I knew from the beginning something that I hid. Virat's death could be the next pandemic for the state.

I knew everything, and it is a long story. Then he even attacked me with the truck. But what happens, happens for good!"

"But…"

"No ifs and buts, just sleep, old man," he interrupted Maisha. "You meet me tomorrow at eight p.m. at the hill."

"Why?"

"I will tell you there!"

"Do you want to kill me also?" said Majid tensely.

"Are you mad? I have some personal work,"

"Ok!" he said in a very scared voice.

They both met at the hill. It was a high point, and much of the city was visible from there. Vikram was sitting on the edge and enjoying the scene.

"Vik- Vikram?" said Majid with a broken voice.

"Oh! Old man, you came. Well, I have some important work!" he replied and took out his gun.

"I didn't do anything, I swear!"

"I know, old man, it is for me!"

"WHAT!"

"Yes, well," he said with a deep and sad voice, "I was not meant for what I have done in my life. Even if people are out for the best, but I have done wrong. I have killed. I broke my mother's promise. I have done so…"

"But…"

"Take this and shoot me!"

"What?" he shouted stiffly. "Are you mad?"

"Well, I was, and now I am perfectly normal!"

"I can't and why would anyone?" he said with a protesting voice.

"Old man, you know everything, well," he said and sighed, "take this and shoot me or I will jump…"

"NO!"

"Then, you kill me. I want to die for the world. I know the world will never find me again. But I have done it. I united them. They are in love, peace, and people are together because of me!"

"Then you stay and do more such things," suggested Majid, and a tear fell from his eye.

"I can't and I won't. Just shoot!"

"But…"

"Old man, do it!"

SHOT!

Epilogue

I sighed when I believed that he was done. It was almost afternoon. My mother called in the middle, but I texted her that I am with a teacher for exams, so do whatever you want to do yourself.

"Well, is it done?" I asked him in hope.

"No, not yet!"

"Then?"

"It is a very long story. Some parts I hid and some are for the future. There are many things that I lied about, but meet me soon and get to know everything."

"When will I meet you again?"

"Any time you like,"

"Can I get your phone number?"

"Yes!"

He gave me his phone number. He sighed and I also did after a moment.

"Well, you said that some parts are missing, which?"

"Well, from the past to future,"

"Well, do you know one thing?"

"What?"

"Well, he was a great man!"

"I know, but no one believes me and no one listens to me. But why did you, and you are so young?"

"Well, age doesn't matter. Well, I was keen, and I knew it is going to be special. Things like this attract me, and I am also of the same mentality."

"Yeah!"

"But isn't he dead, I just remembered?"

*"He died for the **world**," he replied, emphasising the word 'world' more powerfully and smiled. Well, I was confused why he emphasised the word. Maybe it is important.*

"But tell me one thing, why is there no mention of him anywhere?"

"You already know him!"

"What? What do you mean?"

"Yes, he is…"

"Who?"

"Leave it, I was confused,"

"Oh! Then what will be for the future?"

"Well, a very interesting and shocking part!" he replied in a very artistic manner.

"What?"

"Some time else,"

"When?"

"I will tell you," he replied, "you write this and then we will begin another part."

"Ok. Well, I have decided on the title for the story,"

"Really! What?"

"Legend!"

"Well, it suits, and thank you, kid, you are very special!"

"Well, do you know one thing, ah!…"

"RJ,"

"Yes, RJ, but what is your real name?"

"Well, I use RJ but you can call me Jaazib,"

"Ok Jaazib!"

"Yes, please, dear Aryan!"

"There is something very special about you,"

"What?"

"You already know it!"

He laughed, and I also joined him. There was much that awaited me. Well, I believe that the future may be…

"More devastating, deadly, shocking, amusing, interesting, beautiful, and ironical!"

"Really wow! Excited about that. I just want to write about it now!"

"Calm down and be patient,"

"OK, Mister Councillor!"

He again laughed and amused me. He seemed to be an adult, but in reality, he was childish and serious as well.

"Well, I trust you, RJ, so maintain my trust!"

"Koi Shak!"

LEGEND

PART 2: THE WAR

(Jaazib Sheraz)

Coming soon…

"Everything that is hidden and that is missing will be found in another part. Another part is going to be the most shocking thing. Full of misery, violence, treachery, hope and everything. You want to know about the heist, his father, the states, the club, the government, the attacks and some things that are still a mystery. Then stay tuned!"